Holy Land, Holy War

ISAAC YETIV

VANTAGE PRESS
New York / Washington / Atlanta
Los Angeles / Chicago

FIRST EDITION

Published by Vantage Press, Inc.
516 West 34th Street, New York, New York 10001

Manufactured in the United States of America
Standard Book Number 533-03903-7

In memory of
my father,
my mother,
and the innocent victims
of the wars
in the Holy Land

They shall beat their swords into ploughshares, and their spears into pruning-hooks: nation shall not lift up sword against nation, neither shall they learn war any more.

Old Testament, Isaiah, II, 4

The whole Torah exists only for the sake of peace. For the sake of peace, truth may be sacrificed.

Talmud: Gittin 59b; Yevamoth 65b

No one is so foolish as to prefer war to peace in which instead of sons burying their fathers, fathers bury their sons.

Herodotus

Discussion and force are the main ways of settling quarrels, the former of which are peculiar to man, the latter to brute beasts.

Cicero

My first wish is to see this plague of mankind, war, banished from the earth.

Washington

Chapter One

Rabbinas arose that morning a little earlier than usual. The dawn was just beginning to break, and a faint light had already penetrated the half-closed shutters of his bedroom. A feeling of anxiety was troubling him; he had slept badly.

'What have I done?' he wondered. 'I have shared my daily bread with my uncle's widow. I have assisted at our neighbor's wedding, the poor orphan girl. I do not think I have offended the Almighty.' In his community, Rabbinas enjoyed a well-deserved reputation as a just and godly man. "Our fate is in God's hands," he said to himself. "He will in time enlighten us."

With his two hands, he blessed his sleeping children. Then he murmured an appropriate prayer for the safe delivery of his pregnant wife, kissed the *mezuzah*,* and left his house for the synagogue. There he would offer his morning prayer and also attend an urgent meeting called by the President of the Jewish Community.

Rabbinas divided his time between his family, his wholesale-retail grocery store, the synagogue, and the charity work he did to relieve the misery of the poor. His group of friends was a rather narrow one because he was very selective in his choice and valued sincerity and integrity above everything else. Nothing upset him more than unkept promises, slander, and lies. He was undaunted about speaking the truth to the powerful among his coreligionists of whose conduct he disapproved. To support his criticism, he would cite biblical passages and quote them in their original Hebrew to an attentive and

*See glossary of foreign words and expressions, p. 121.

1

dumbfounded congregation. Isaiah and Amos were his favorite prophets because they decried social injustice and defended the wretched, the orphans, and the widows.

Rabbinas's company was sought out by the young students who came to spend their summer vacations with their families in the little Mediterranean town of Neapolis in Tunisia. The grocery store was located in the heart of the town. Rabbinas had been conducting his business for almost thirty years. As young children, the students used to come to stock up on candy or to pick up items their mothers had forgotten to buy. It was the children who had bestowed on this fatherlike figure the nickname of Rabbinas—a nice contraction of Rabbi Pinhas, as he was called at the synagogue.

At the store entrance were three chairs, one for Rabbinas and the others for his frequent visitors. Very seldom were these chairs empty. Most often the store was packed, not with shoppers but with student-philosophers as these strange customers proudly called themselves. They would bring him their freshly acquired "science," talking about Marx and the exploitation of the workers. Rabbinas would smile and often reply, "There is nothing new under the sun, so spoke King Solomon. This gentleman Marx has invented nothing; all this is in the Bible." And he would cite from memory entire Hebrew chapters, which he translated into Arabic as he proceeded: about the law that required an employer to pay his workers from day to day; about the Sabbath, the mandatory weekly day of rest for all; and about the imperative commandment to care for the stranger, the widow, and the orphan. Isaiah and Amos were always mentioned as the social reformers who preached twenty-five centuries before Marx.

The young, even the most radical among them, were fascinated by his broad knowledge. They admired his prodigious memory. They respected him for his convictions and, even more, for living according to his beliefs and in harmony with his principles.

The Jewish students were not the only true friends of Rabbinas. Friday, market day in Neapolis, was reserved for the "old wise men," the Arab notables who came from neighboring villages to shop for their families or for their own small markets. They made their long journey by horse-drawn carriage or on a donkey. The most regular among them was Sheik Sliman; he had not missed a single Friday in twenty years.

In the store, only a few minutes were devoted to business. Contrary to the practice in these parts, the Arab notables would not discuss prices with Rabbinas. Absolute confidence was the rule on both sides; it was strengthened by long, unblemished experience and by sincere mutual respect. The rest of the time was for philosophizing, the conversation proceeding in Arabic.

Rabbinas was well acquainted with the language; he had even published a few poems and funereal orations in Judeo-Arabic, using the Hebrew alphabet to transcribe the Arabic dialect. The discussions dealt with God, the Creation, man, and man's duty toward his neighbor. A preliminary agreement was tacitly reached between Rabbinas and Sheik Sliman: they acknowledged the fact that they were different. Rabbinas was a Jew; Sheik Sliman, a Moslem. They respected each other's religious beliefs, and in their intellectual debates they sought the common ground in the dogmas and practices of Judaism and Islam.

Actually, the common ground was not hard to find. Weren't Isaac and Ishmael sons of the same father, Abraham? Weren't Arabic and Hebrew sister Semitic languages? Both Jews and Moslems, shouldn't they pray, fast, and practice charity? And most importantly, didn't they believe in the same one God, Elohim or Allah?

During these conversations, they enjoyed comparing verses from the Bible and the Koran. One day, Sheik Sliman, amazed at the almost identical teachings of both religions, exclaimed: "But why? Why more than one religion for all of us?" Then he reflected and added: "God is one and eternal, and it is He, blessed be His Name, who created men different and religions different. We must respect His will."

Rabbinas concurred: "Yes, God is one and eternal, and we

are all His creatures. All men are equal in the eyes of God because they are all created in His image."

Discussing religion was not their only activity. Often they played games, and one of the most captivating was the riddle. Between two Fridays, one of them would make up a verse riddle and recite it to the other, allowing him one or two weeks to think it over and find the solution. According to the rules of the game, each could ask the other for only one clue: Is it God's creation or a man-made object? Rabbinas and Sheik Sliman had exercised their minds to such a high degree that it was rare that either of them drew a blank on a riddle.

One day, Sheik Sliman arrived beaming and called out from afar, "Rabbinas, my friend, I brought something great for you; you'll have four weeks to guess the answer!"

The old man greeted him cheerfully, then said, "I am all ears. Is it created by God or made by man?"

The Sheik provided the mandatory clue: "It is God's creation," and proceeded with his riddle:

> His eyes look without pleasure;
> How strong the poor man's grief!
> He resembles the one who fasts in summer:
> He thirsts and yet water is within his reach.

Rabbinas asked his friend to repeat it a second time while he took notes and then a third time to check what he wrote; then he congratulated him for the beauty and harmony of the verses and promised to do his best.

When his time was up, Rabbinas offered several possible answers which Sheik Sliman rejected one after the other, though he admitted that two of them came very close. After the last unsuccessful guess, Rabbinas gave up, and his friend announced, "It's a eunuch, Rabbinas! You must know that in the days of Harun El-Rashid, the Emir had his wives escorted to the bath by a eunuch slave whose mission was to make sure that no other men came near the women. The Emir didn't worry about the eunuchs since they were sexually harmless. Quite often, however, these eunuchs were men who had tasted of love before being castrated; despite their impotence, they coveted the beautiful naked females confided to their care, just as the one who fasts desires the water placed before him without being able to quench his thirst."

Rabbinas examined his friend's solution to the riddle for a moment to make sure that no piece of the puzzle was missing. Then, convinced, he said, "Bravo, Sheik Sliman! It is perfect, nicely put together. Today I learned something."

But the old Sheik, as if apologizing, responded, "Of course, this situation is foreign to Jewish customs."

"No, not at all," replied Rabbinas. "The book of Esther mentions eunuchs quite often, and though it refers to Persia, I should have thought of that. I don't mean, however, that I would have gotten the answer."

The conversation then turned to Persia and to Queen Esther, who saved her people from extermination at the hands of the wicked Haman, and to the God of Israel who always sends a savior to rescue his people.

Chapter Two

As he was leaving his house, Rabbinas remembered this conversation with his friend. A freezing wind whistled across his face. Along the way, he couldn't help repeating mentally the names of Esther and Haman. Each time the latter resounded in his mind, Rabbinas shuddered because he couldn't forget that over across the Mediterranean, there in Europe, another Haman, more modern in his technique of extermination, had already arisen and was hell-bent on the diabolical enterprise of the earlier tyrant. There was talk of concentration camps and crematoria, the monstrous means to carry out Hitler's "final solution" to the Jewish problem: total extermination.

Rabbinas himself had seen pictures of white-bearded rabbis wrapped in their prayer shawls, who were led to the slaughter with the name of God on their lips. He began to feel ashamed: ashamed of not being able to do anything; ashamed of living a sheltered life while there, in Europe, his people was being massacred; ashamed of not sharing the dangers his brothers in Europe were facing in a war which was a European affair so far from his own country; ashamed of God's refusal to accept his prayers, the prayers of Pinhas the Righteous, and save his people.

As always, he concluded his meditations with a verse of consolation. This time he murmured in Hebrew: "In each generation, they rise up to wipe us out, and God, blessed be his name, delivers us from their hands." Then he turned his steps toward the Temple which was already filled with people.

6

The pressing matter, he was told, was to welcome and provide shelter for three Jewish families who had escaped from the European hell. These families were already there, and Rabbinas greeted the frightened group of fugitives. Their empty and frozen gaze spoke at length of the sufferings they had endured for the five months of their forced journey. They had left occupied France, walking as far as the Spanish border. After they had spent a long while in Spain, an American philanthropic organization took charge of them and placed them on a cargo ship bound for Tunisia. At the end of a long and perilous voyage, they landed at Tunis and were immediately sent to Neapolis to the care of the small Jewish community which thus contributed its modest share to the rescue operation.

The refugees had nothing more than the clothes on their back; some of them were even in rags. The children trembled with fear and chattered their teeth. Only the mothers, resigned to their fate, seemed quiet and thankful to their helping brothers.

"Dear Lord," said Rabbinas to himself, "are you going to send us another Esther to destroy this new Haman?"

The divine response was not long in coming: a horrible cry broke through the silence: "The Germans are coming!"

It was the raucous voice of a member of the rescue committee who had come late to the reception center because he had been riveted to his radio set listening to the latest reports. "This time, it's for real; we're doomed," he added. "This war is no longer a European affair. The same destiny awaits us here, the destiny of our brothers in Europe. Where can we go from here? Who will welcome us?"

This alarming news cast fear and consternation over the crowd. The hosts were at bay; the dismayed guests, desperate. Rabbinas remained calm. He would no longer feel shame; from now on, he would suffer like his brothers. But the reality suddenly struck him, and he realized the extent of the calamity that had befallen his community.

A few hours later, Nazi troops marched down the streets of Neapolis, and the town walls were covered with giant posters proclaiming in big print: "The war was wanted and prepared for by international Jewry. That is why I decided to inflict on the community a fine of twenty million francs." It was signed: General von Harnim.

Local government was suspended. From that moment on, everything would be decided by the Kommandantur, the German military headquarters. Decrees discriminating against the Jews were quickly promulgated. Not only did they have to pay the collective fine, but every Jew had to wear an armband to distinguish him from the rest of the population. Either out of ignorance or scorn, the armband was a blue Star of David on a white background, a real Jewish flag. It was a slight change from the yellow star imposed upon the European Jews, but it remained, just the same, a distinctive mark which allowed the occupiers to round up Jews whenever they wished.

Jews were banned from any public function, from education, from banks. Many of them returned to their fathers' trades as carpenters, shoemakers, or tailors. The racist measures didn't stop at that. The order came to send Jews between eighteen and forty years of age to forced labor camps to build bridges and airfields, and the community had to supply the manpower and provide for a meager subsistence of the poor workers.

Some of the younger members of the community suggested resisting and disobeying the German orders, but the majority decided to meet the ruthless occupiers' demands in order to avoid the worst. There were very few losses in human life, and these deaths were due mainly to accidents.

Detailed plans for the construction of a crematorium were ready, but they weren't implemented for lack of time. As in Europe, the Germans were intent on achieving the "final solution" for the Tunisian Jewish community.

On that somber day, Rabbinas opened his store a little later than usual because of the events and also because he had to take care of the refugees. He was surprised to find his old friend sitting on the elevated threshold, patiently waiting for him. "Sheik Sliman!" he exclaimed. "You are always welcome. I am very pleased to see you, but today . . . it is not Friday."

8

The quiet and long answer seemed to have been carefully prepared: "Rabbinas, my friend, our friendship has been unmarred during all these years. I have just heard that the Germans are here. I don't know whether I should rejoice at the defeat of the French, with whom we have a long account to settle, or fear the victory of these barbaric people who, every day, kill innocent human beings by the thousands. I was ashamed to hear that some of my fellow Arabs serve as guides to the Germans and lead them to Jewish homes. I have decided to come here very early this morning to make sure that you are not hurt and to pledge my honor that, as long as Sheik Sliman lives, no one will dare harm Rabbinas and his family."

Rabbinas was very moved by this show of human warmth and generosity. He was aware of the dangers that his friend would risk by challenging the Germans' authority and obstructing their "justice." He hesitated a moment to ponder his words. "Sheik Sliman," he said with emotion, "God has sent you; may God bless you!"

As they spoke, an unruly crowd gathered in the public square, yelling anti-French and anti-Jewish slogans and acclaiming their German liberators at the top of their voices. Bloody threats were uttered against the few Jews who still walked in the street. The old Sheik cast a fearful glance around him and advised his companion to close the store and go home to his family. "In two or three days, the frenzy will die down," he said. "Please allow me to accompany you."

As they drew closer, Rabbinas was astonished to see, in front of his house, a group of Arabs gesticulating and pointing out the door to two German soldiers. For the first time, he felt fear and began to worry about his two sons of labor-camp age. When he could distinguish the faces, he saw that they were strangers to his neighborhood. He was confident that the town Arabs who knew him well and respected him would never do that.

All of a sudden, he heard a shout from beside him: "Be off with you!" yelled Sheik Sliman. "Return to your homes immediately! What have these people done to you? Fear Allah!"

9

Luckily, they were people from his own village. They bowed their heads in shame and took off immediately.

Chapter Three

The midwife left the bedroom, smiling. "It's a boy!" she told Rabbinas who was absorbed in his reading of the Psalms. "The baby is well, and the mother, too."

"God be praised!" said Rabbinas and he immediately began to think of the circumcision rite.

It was a few days before Passover, the Passover of 1943, which promised to be dark and painful. Nearly five months had slipped by since that November day marked by the arrival of the Germans and the unexpected visit of Sheik Sliman. The restrictions and privations had become more and more difficult to endure. Food supplies were not to be found since the country first had to feed the German army. Even bread was scarce, except on the black market at exorbitant prices which only the wealthy could afford.

Rabbinas's family never lacked bread. Every day, an anonymous messenger knocked discreetly at their door and, out of a large basket, took two fresh loaves of bread which he delivered without saying a word. Rabbinas had no doubts about the identity of his benefactor. It was Sheik Sliman for sure, God's emissary, who provided for the family needs. "There is nothing lost in this world," he said to himself. "A good deed is never forgotten; God always repays us in kind. When I gave the widow her daily bread, I never imagined that God would one day reward me and provide for my own bread. But how stupid I am! How many times have I repeated King Solomon's words: 'Cast your bread on the water; one day you will recover it.'"

The daily hardships were not the only source of sadness in the Rabbinas household. His two grown sons were away. The older had been rounded up by the Germans the first week of the occupation, and news from him was scarce. They only knew that he was working at a military airfield and that he had miraculously escaped death during intense bombing by Allied airplanes. As for the younger, he had been able, with the help of his father's friends, to hide out in a farm where he was safe from the Germans. A comforting short message reached his father every Friday, brought by his faithful customers.

Rabbinas often remembered his older sons' circumcisions. On the eve of the ceremony, the house was full of guests. They served drinks; they ate, sang, and read prayers; they wished good health to the mother, and a life full of *mitsvot*, of good deeds, to the newborn. The next day, the *mohel* came to circumcise the baby and thus seal the eternal bond between God and Abraham.

"This time, it will be very different," Rabbinas told his wife. "It is not a time for celebrations; we will simply perform the religious rite, and the *minyan* of the synagogue will suffice. We must find a name for the child which will remind us of the present situation and the circumstances of his birth."

"What do you think of Moshe?" asked his wife. "It is the name of your uncle who died last year, and it also suggests Passover, the holiday of freedom."

"But that might not be wise," answered Rabbinas. "It will be construed as an act of provocation against the Germans and their subservient collaborators. We will call him *Rahamim*, Mercy. May God accept our prayer and have *mercy* on us."

The ceremony took place on the eighth day after the birth, and the benediction, read by Rabbinas himself, ended with the words: "He shall be named Rahamim ben Pinhas Levy."

Chapter Four

Amin Ibn-Hussein was one of the most violent soldiers of Fawzi El Kaukdji. With his oldest son, he had enlisted in the Kaukdji battalion of snipers, and his mission was to shoot up Jewish vehicles on the road connecting Tel Aviv to Jerusalem. He had left his wife and two younger sons to work the farm which he owned at Om-el-Kokeb. He had for pay his daily food ration, some cigarettes, and a little spending money. What truly motivated him was his strong hatred of Jews and the hope of getting part of the booty when the last of the Jews—"the children of death" as he called them—would be hurled into the sea. He had already picked out his house in Tel-Aviv, a city he knew quite well. And he wasn't slow in spotting two pretty young Jewish women whom he would own after the final victory.

In the meantime, one of his two wives at home, Zohra, was well on her way to enlarging his family. Her pregnancy, however, did not prevent her from plowing and watering the fields, milking the cows, taking care of the hen house, drawing water from far-off wells, and carrying rather heavy loads at arm's length or on her head. At home, three children awaited her. She had to return home several times a day in order to nurse the smallest one and to give the others something to eat. Zohra also had the task of selling farm produce at the neighboring town market. Amin would come once a week to get the money from the sale of the milk and eggs, leaving his wife a little cash for her daily expenses.

The second wife, Salha, led a life very much the same, and

13

Amin shared his visits between the two women who got along rather well and were resigned to their fate. Their submissiveness to their common husband and the vicissitudes of daily life had brought together these rival wives who, under other circumstances, would have been enemies. In this part of the world, tradition made the woman an object which the man manipulated at will. None dreamed of revolting and changing this state of affairs. Some young men of the village would dare from time to time to express their discontent, but their timid protest was always squelched by their elders who accused them of wanting to abjure Islam and the teachings of the Prophet and follow the example of the impious foreigners who came to steal their lands and corrupt their morals. They were alluding to European Jews who were living in Tel Aviv or at the neighboring kibbutz.

Certain relationships existed between the two communities, and young liberal Arabs looked with envy at the Jewish women who were free and emancipated. They admired their intelligence, their modern style of dress, and their role in the community. They watched them on the beaches in bathing suits, while their mothers and sisters suffocated under black dresses which covered them from head to toe.

Amin was well aware of the unrest of the youth. He had worked with the "Zionists" and knew their customs. He often coveted their women but shuddered at the thought that his wives or his daughters would follow the example of these Jewish women of loose morals and would want to wear shorts or speak privately with a man. "God spare us from this calamity," Amin would often say to his son, who seemed to pity the lot of the women in his village. "Better die than let our wives become corrupted like these prostitutes, these daughters of the devil whom God will soon help us wipe out with their males who have no honor and dignity."

One day, harassed by questions from his younger son, Amin confessed to him, "This war is going to be a *jihad*, a holy war as our *Mufti* has declared it. And with the help of God, we will extirpate from our body this cancer which threatens to destroy us." Then, as if about to set his diabolical plan in motion, he reloaded his rifle and returned to the fields to rejoin his company of snipers posted along the winding road which led to Jerusalem.

Chapter Five

It was night in the camp, and only a faint light illuminated the mustachioed faces of Kaukdji's soldiers. A large pot of coffee was heating over a fire, which had been camouflaged so as not to draw the attention of the Jewish convoy. Amin rolled a cigarette and awaited the order that would allow him to shoot at the vehicles carrying men and supplies to Jerusalem. "May they all die," he said aloud. "Allah is with us!" He raised his head and saw in the distance a human silhouette running towards the camp. Instinctively he grabbed his rifle and yelled, "Who goes there?" An adolescent's voice answered from the distance. He recognized the voice of one of his two sons, who was supposed to be in the village with Zohra. He thanked God that he hadn't fired.

"My mother sent me to tell you that she is having labor pains and to ask you to come right away," said the young man. At first, Amin wanted to refuse; his duty was to stay with his comrades-in-arms. But his commander intervened and ordered him to go home and to come back two days after the delivery. Amin muttered a few words against this woman who was preventing him from killing Jews on the night he was sure to do some butchering. Then, grumbling, he took his son's hand and headed towards the farm.

Fatima emerged from the corner of the big room where, behind a curtain, Zohra had just uttered her last scream after a night of horrible suffering.

16

"I have attended the birth of all of your children, Amin, and I have helped Zohra in all of her deliveries," said the old midwife, whose reputation in the village was unblemished. "This time it was different. The devil had a hand in it, I'm sure, or some wicked sorceress. Zohra lost a lot of blood. She died from it, Amin. God wanted it that way. She gave you a daughter. Salha is now washing and clothing her."

"Let God's will be done," said Amin. "Zohra was a godly and hardworking woman; she never complained. May God rest her soul."

It was with great regret that Amin decided not to return to his unit, but to stay in the village with his family and help Salha raise the little girl.

"What are you going to call her?" Salha asked him.

"Jihada," came the prompt reply. Amin seemed to have prepared it long before.

"Jihada!" Salha exclaimed. "I have never heard such a name."

"That's true," said Amin. "Since I have to give up the *jihad*, the holy war against the Jews—may God annihilate them—my daughter will carry this name all her life and will always remind me of my sacred duty to destroy these impious enemies of our people."

"Jihada! Jihada!" repeated Salha incredulously as she left the room.

Chapter Six

Rahamim Levy was a month old when the Germans were driven out of Tunisia. On the eighth of May, 1943, the radio announced the liberation of Neapolis. The Jewish population was ecstatic. "Once again, God has sent us a savior," Rabbinas said to his wife. "This time His messenger is the British army. We must never despair, for, as our Fathers say, divine succor comes in the twinkling of an eye."

As soon as the news was announced, all Jews left their homes and gathered in a huge crowd to celebrate the liberation. Some British armored cars were stormed by the excited masses. Everybody hugged and kissed. British soldiers were hoisted on the shoulders of men, and the air filled with cries of "Long live England! . . . Long live France! . . . Long live the Allies!" And there were cries of hatred and vengeance against certain French collaborators and certain Arabs accused of denouncing Jews to the Germans.

Among the celebrators, a face seemed to have risen from the dead. It was Zakshi; he had been thought dead or captive but, in fact, he had been hiding from the Germans in the wooden box of the upholstered divan of his living room. He had been drafted in 1939 and sent to the French front. During the rout of the French army, he had been made a prisoner by the Germans but had succeeded in escaping and returning to his family. With the occupation of Tunisia, he couldn't go any farther and his courageous father had decided to hide him out in the divan. Some holes had been bored in the wood in order to let him breathe, and twice a day, after having carefully bolted the door and the windows, his father would raise the cushioning in order to give him food and water.

Now, standing in front of a dumfounded crowd, surrounded by his elated friends, Zakshi enjoyed his regained freedom. He told them how, several times, the Germans had come to search his house and how his father had had them calmly sit on the divan while he himself struggled, his heart pounding, to hold his breath.

The day of the liberation, his father paid a visit to Rabbinas and asked him to compose a prayer of thanks to the God of Israel. Later, this prayer became the official one in all synagogues. The Jewish community praised God and blessed the instrument of his vengeance, the British army.

Arabs didn't venture into the streets. Many of them had staked everything on a German victory. Some even had gone so far as to enlist in the German army and parade in the streets in Nazi uniform. A few fled with the retreating Wehrmacht, fearing arrest as traitors and collaborators.

Sheik Sliman stayed away for two Fridays in a row, and Rabbinas went to see him in his own village in order to tell him that their friendship had not changed. "The Germans have come and gone, the English also will go, but we always remain in this land. You were very good to us during the German occupation, Sheik Sliman. You did everything to comfort us. British law is a just law. It only punishes the guilty. You have nothing to fear, nothing to hide; I can attest to that."

The following Friday, Sheik Sliman repaid Rabbinas's visit, and their intellectual conversations were resumed.

The Judeo-British honeymoon was very brief. The British attitude toward Palestinian Jews turned the world public opinion against them. The scandal of *Exodus 47*, the ship filled with survivors of concentration camps which the British prevented from landing at Haifa, made headlines for a long while. It was a stiff blow to British prestige and to their reputation as a civilized people. They were inevitably compared to the Nazis. They were accused of favoring the Arabs and preventing the establishment of an independent Jewish state.

For Tunisian Jews, the liberator had now become the hated persecutor. In Palestine terrorist Jewish organizations swore to rid the country of its foreign oppressor. They increased their strikes, and in so doing showed determination and courage, a powerful imagination and an ingenious mind. An army of 100,000 English soldiers was unable to control these groups which had the material and moral support of the Jewish communities and a great deal of world sympathy on their side.

Exhausted, the British Government turned to the United Nations which adopted a resolution to create two independent states, one Jewish and one Arab. This was a historic decision; after twenty centuries of wandering and persecution, the Jewish people were at last about to gain national sovereignty in their ancestral homeland. The Jewish population of Palestine was enthralled. People danced and kissed in the streets of Tel Aviv. But their political leaders were worried by the bellicose declarations of their neighbors. They knew very well that political recognition and moral support meant absolutely nothing without the military power to defend their newly acquired independence. The Arab leaders never accepted the idea of an independent Jewish state which they saw as "a thorn in their flesh." They decided to nip it in the bud and called for a *jihad*. Kaukdji's snipers gave way to regular armies from Arab countries which encircled the tiny new-born state of Israel. Fighting for its survival, Israel mobilized all its men and women capable of bearing arms.

Chapter Seven

"Soldiers of Israel, the enemy has sworn to throw us into the sea. Seven Arab states threaten us with extinction. They have the advantage of numbers and supplies. We have already suffered heavy casualties, but we have no alternative but to fight because our very existence is at stake. Our courage and our sacrifices will determine the outcome of this war which has been forced upon us. We must at any price win this war. Our young men are fighting and dying on all fronts. Our mission today is to drive away the enemy from Om-el-Kokeb and take this plateau. Have courage and good luck!"

The commander had ended his short speech, and the officers were already organizing their troops. Some soldiers were cleaning their rifles; others were hastily writing a postcard, perhaps their last, to their families. Alone in a corner, Mendel Weiss was ruminating. He was passing before his mind's eye the last years of his life: his deportation in 1942 to Auschwitz until his liberation; his decision to get to Palestine on a boat of illegal immigrants; his stay in a kibbutz; his military training which he completed as a sergeant commanding a small infantry unit that was to lead the assault on Om-el-Kokeb. At the kibbutz, Mendel had left his girl friend, Gita. She, too, was a victim of the Nazis. They had strong ties of friendship and they promised to remain friends if he came out of the war alive. She confessed to him one day that the Germans had mutilated her, that they had performed biological experiments on her body and that she would never be able to bear children. This intimacy

21

brought him closer to Gita, and he regarded her with a mixture of pity and admiration. His entire family had perished in Auschwitz, and Gita was the only person in the world he loved and cared for. 'Would he ever see her again,' he wondered.

His commander called him and cut short his reverie. He briefly described his mission. The sergeant gathered his men and repeated the last orders, stressing the importance of the military operations on the Eastern front and their impact on the broader issue of the conflict.

A few minutes later, the whole convoy was on its way. There was almost no Arab resistance. Sergeant Weiss's unit successfully accomplished its mission. His men had only to mop up a few houses inside the village.

It was dark and, from afar, very difficult to tell one thing from another. Mendel asked his second in command, who spoke Arabic, to urge the civilian population, through the loudspeaker, to leave their homes and gather in the public square in order to avoid unnecessary loss of life. But this proved useless; no one emerged from the houses. "They must be crazy," Mendel said. "Or maybe there are hidden soldiers who refuse to surrender."

He split his unit into groups of two and ordered them to search every house and not to fire unless attacked first. He himself headed towards one of the houses. It was completely silent. On entering, he noticed some kitchen utensils strewn on the floor, and in a corner, two sheepskins and some charcoal embers still smoldering in a clay stove. Not too far from the fireplace, an overturned teapot was half-full of still warm tea. In the yard, a dog barked and two chickens pecked away at some feed.

Mendel cautiously entered one of the bedrooms. The beds were unmade, and clothes were strewn about helter-skelter in a closet which seemed to have been emptied of its most precious contents. Mendel was now certain of what had happened: the village inhabitants must certainly have fled from the victorious Jewish army; they were well acquainted with the field paths leading to Jordanian territory.

The sergeant was getting ready to send his report to his commander when he suddenly heard a child's cry coming from the next room. He held his breath to make sure that the cry was real. Then he put off his message for later and quickly entered the room. He saw nothing. Again, the cry. Mendel drew nearer to the bed, and his doubts vanished; the cry came from underneath the bed. He turned back the wool blanket that covered it and hung down to the floor. He bent over for a second and shone his flashlight into the darkest corners.

A strong wave of emotion made him shudder. He was gripped by a trembling which swept over his entire body. Cowering in a corner, a little baby a few months old was staring at him. The baby was dirty and seemed hungry.

"It's a girl," said Weiss to his buddy. "Unbelievable! How could they forget their child? They must have looked for it a long while before giving up. How come she is under the bed?"

He added to his report a few sentences telling about his strange discovery and asking for orders from his superior. A few minutes later, the officer replied: "Turn the baby over to the civilian authorities of the town." Mendel took pity on the child. He spotted a bucket of water in the yard, took a piece of soap out of his bag, and began washing the baby who never stopped crying. Then he asked one of his comrades to dissolve some powdered milk in water and to warm the mixture on a nearby stove. There was no bottle, and he had to feed the baby with a spoon. Mendel found this task rather comforting. The child had a tremendous appetite. When Mendel put the last spoonful to her mouth, it was closed. The infant was already sleeping in his arms.

"Poor innocent one," murmured the sergeant. "Poor victim of man's cruelty." Instinctively he closed his eyes to spare himself the frightful picture of other children in Europe who were torn from the arms of their mothers and taken to their death. "God, how wicked men are! How mean the human animal is!" he cried. Then he gently kissed the baby's tender cheek.

Suddenly some soldiers burst into the house. Their job was to search for important military documents and to uncover hid-

23

den weapons. They were surprised to see a baby in the arms of a fellow soldier. Weiss told them the story very briefly and let them continue their search. He was about to leave when one of the soldiers ran over to him with papers written in Arabic. They were family identification documents with the names and ages of the whole family; on the first page, was a picture of a mustachioed man wearing *kefia* on his head. To the right of the picture was his name in large Arabic letters: Amin Ibn-Hussein. Mendel snatched the booklet from the soldier's hand and turned the pages rapidly until he got to the last one. "Here it is!" he said to the soldier. "Read me this quickly." He couldn't wait any longer; he wanted to know the name of the little girl whose life he had just saved.

The soldier paused a moment. Then, astonished, he yelled, "Jihada! What a name! Born the fourteenth of April, 1948. I've never heard such a name. It must mean something special."

"What?" inquired the sergeant anxiously.

"I can only tell you what *jihad* means. To the best of my knowledge . . ."

"What?" interrupted Weiss, more impatient.

"It's the holy war of the Moslems against the infidels," the soldier coldly replied and returned to his search.

"Jihada Ibn-Hussein! Jihada! Jihada!" repeated Mendel as he left the house to take the baby to the civilian authorities.

The village square was deserted; not a soul in the cafés. The administrative offices were closed or empty; the Arab civil servants must have hastily left their jobs and fled with their families. Weiss did not know what to do with Jihada. His commanding officer could not be found; he was probably on a military mission somewhere. The war was not over; Mendel knew that other battles lay ahead and that he could not drag the baby along with him. He had to get rid of this strange burden, but what was he to do? He couldn't abandon her in the street; that would condemn the child to a sure death.

One idea crossed his mind: he'd go to the kibbutz and leave Jihada in Gita's hands until . . . He didn't know how to end his thought. There were too many unknowns in this bizarre situ-

24

ation: Gita wasn't his wife. How would the kibbutz react? And who knew if he would come back alive from the war? But he cut short his meanderings. 'That's what I've got to do,' he decided. 'There's nothing else.' He had a few hours off until the next battle order. He jumped into his jeep, made a U-turn around the square, and headed for the kibbutz. Jihada was still asleep beside him.

Surprised, Gita welcomed him. She was happy to see him safe and sound because she had just read an army communiqué relating heavy casualties. Weiss was very embarrassed; he didn't know how to begin and what Gita would say.

"Here is a little Arab girl," he muttered. "Her name is Jihada. I . . . we found her almost dead under a bed in one of the Arab houses. I couldn't let her die. We washed her, and fed her, and . . . here she is." He was awkwardly aware that he hadn't asked Gita to keep the child and that he was waiting for her reaction.

"But," she stammered, "do we have the right? Won't there be anyone to claim her? And the kibbutz, how will they take it?"

"There was no one left in town; everybody had fled. Gita, I beg you to understand. Help me keep the baby here until . . ."

"Until what?"

Jihada opened her eyes, and her gaze met Gita's. "What beautiful dark eyes," Gita said in a pathetic voice. "I don't know what it is, but I have a strange feeling for this child, a sort of affection, as if she were my own daughter."

Mendel breathed deeply; he was relieved. "I must rejoin my unit," he said. He took Jihada in his arms and kissed her strongly. He hugged his faithful girl friend to him and their lips touched.

"You know," he said when he released his grasp, "for the first time in my life, I have a feeling of being separated from my family."

"See you soon," answered Gita, stifling a sob. "We will wait for you."

The military hospital was crowded. Every hour, ambulances brought their load of wounded soldiers. The doctors who were called up worked day and night, and nurses went from one wounded man to another, taking temperatures, giving injections, feeding those who couldn't help themselves, and comforting parents. It was a terrible sight.

On the first floor, surgeons operated on the critically wounded. Entire families waited in the corridors. Pious men prayed or read verses from the Psalms. Gita remained silent in a corner and waited patiently. She had gotten a telegram that contained the terrible news: "Mendel Weiss seriously wounded." She was listed as his next-of-kin, as his only "relative," and she was asked to come to the hospital. For three long hours, she had been waiting for the outcome of the operation.

"He's out of danger," said the surgeon, opening the door at last. "He lost one of his lungs, but he will leave the hospital soon. He is lucky."

Gita thanked the doctor and asked if she could see her friend. "Not before tomorrow," he answered. "He needs rest. Please come back tomorrow morning."

She left the hospital and went back to the kibbutz. A few weeks had gone by since the day she had last seen him, the same day she had seen Jihada for the first time. She couldn't sleep a wink that night. She knew that military doctors would tell the truth in similar circumstances and she believed that Mendel was out of danger. But she feared unforeseen complications and shook at the idea of never seeing him alive again. 'It isn't only for myself,' she thought. 'but also—and particularly—for the baby.'

The next day Mendel welcomed her with a smile. He was very pale and weak, and the doctors had restricted Gita's visit to a few minutes.

"Thanks for coming," he said in a whisper. "And thanks for all that you have done for Jihada. How is the little girl? How was she received by the kibbutz?"

Gita had anticipated the questions with apprehension and

26

she avoided a direct answer. "Everything's fine," she said. "And you? How are you feeling? How were you wounded? Where?"

Mendel persisted; only one thing interested him: "Ji-ha-da! Please tell me about her, please, Gita."

"I told you that everything's fine now," said Gita. "There were certain obstacles which I managed to overcome. At my request, the adoption committee of the kibbutz met to decide the fate of the little one. I suggested that the kibbutz temporarily adopt her until . . ."

"Until!" Mendel cut in, echoing another conversation with Gita.

"Until you return home from the front," she said forcefully. "Opinions differed. Some members of the committee supported my request, but the majority were against it, and I must admit that their arguments carried weight. They said that it wasn't only a human problem, but that this question raised tremendous legal difficulties, and that the kibbutz could not become involved in what might be considered an abduction. I explained your position—our position—I said that you did your best to follow your commanding officer's orders, that you tried to turn her over to the Arab civilian authorities, but that you could find no one. Our friend Dahlia came to my help, adding: 'He couldn't just leave her to die in the street. Would that have been more humane?' "

"And then?" said Mendel, eager to know the rest.

"They decided after a long debate to keep her temporarily at the kibbutz until . . ."

"Until my return from the war?" inquired Mendel with hope.

"No!" replied Gita. "Until they find her parents."

"What parents?" yelled Mendel. "We are her par. . . ."

"Mendel! Please, take it easy. You're not well yet."

"No, Gita. It's more than I can stand; I can't take it any more. Without me this child would be dead. The parents? They are the ones who love, care for, and raise the child, not those who abandon her. I am the girl's father. I will make her my daughter, le-gal-ly if they want me to. And you, Gita, my faithful friend, my only friend in the whole world, I ask you here and now to become her mother. She will not be an orphan. She will have a mother and a father."

"I will do anything . . . to keep the baby," Gita replied with tears in her eyes.

The idea of adopting Jihada had remained with her from the moment Mendel left the baby in her care. She knew that she was sterile, and Mendel knew it, too. She found herself in a delicate situation because her desire to have the child adopted by the kibbutz had already been interpreted by some as a trick which would allow her later on to become her mother. Furthermore, she had been completely unaware of Mendel's real intentions. They had been intimate for two years, yet the word *marriage* had never been mentioned. She had always thought that Mendel didn't want a childless marriage. Now things changed; they had the same views and the same intentions. Mendel had just proposed marriage and the legal adoption of the child.

When she calmed down, Gita wiped her wet cheeks and continued in a hardly perceptive voice: "Yes, Mendel, I will be your wife."

"Thank you, Gita," Mendel answered, reassured. "As soon as I get out of here, I'll take care of the formalities. Nobody will take Jihada from me."

"No, not Jihada! Her name is Shlomit now," said Gita. "The kibbutz decided to rename her Shlomit. They thought that Jihada was an Arab name with a warlike meaning and, not knowing exactly how long her temporary stay at the kibbutz would last, they thought it better to give her a Hebrew name and save her from difficulties in the future. Someone suggested the name Shlomit as an antithesis to Jihada, and everybody accepted it."

"Shlomit!" repeated Mendel. "Peace! Peace!"

Chapter Eight

The Jewish population of Neapolis passionately followed the events in Palestine. The weekly gazette brought fresh news of victories and also of setbacks. The most painful was the loss of the old city of Jerusalem. No one could be sure of the outcome of the fight, and all were fearful of a catastrophe which would lead not only to the annihilation of the Jewish population in Palestine, as its enemies had sworn, but would also put an end to the two-thousand-year-old dream of the rebuilding of Zion. Some families in Neapolis feared for their own children who had volunteered to defend the beleaguered young state. David Levy was among them. He was the oldest of Rabbinas's children, and his father had not received news of him for three months.

Sheik Sliman came to see Rabbinas one day. He had learned from the Arabs in his village that Rabbinas's son had gone to Palestine to kill Arabs.

"Is it true?" asked Sheik Sliman.

"Only half," answered Rabbinas. "It is true that he has gone to Palestine. But to defend his people, not to kill Arabs."

Sheik Sliman didn't seem convinced. Nevertheless, he listened patiently. "I had a long talk with David," Rabbinas went on. " 'Father,' he told me, 'you remember when the Germans rounded me up and sent me for six months of forced labor on an airfield. Like a slave or a criminal, I toiled while the bombs exploded all around. I came out of it unharmed, thank God, but six million Jews in Europe couldn't make it, and were

29

slaughtered. This massacre must not be repeated in the Holy Land. You are the one who taught me to say: 'If I forget thee, O Jerusalem, may my right hand wither away from me!' Today, Father, Jerusalem is in great danger. How can I forget her? I feel that it is my duty to join these heroic fighters.' " Then, after a pause, Rabbinas added, "So I put my two hands on his head and I blessed him: 'May you go in peace, my son, and may you return in peace!' But David looked me straight in the eye and replied: 'No, Father, whatever happens, I will never come back!' "

Sheik Sliman was visibly moved. He sighed deeply and said with relief mixed with bitterness, "I am glad, Rabbinas, that I do not have a son. Who knows, he too might have decided, like some boys of my village, to fight at the side of the Arabs. God preserve us! My son killing the son of Rabbinas or being killed by him! I understand nothing any more, Rabbinas, everything is all confused. Where is reason? Where is truth? If we are friends, why are our peoples enemies? What force is pushing us to hate one another? God . . ."

Rabbinas didn't let him complete his sentence to spare him a blasphemy: "No, Sheik Sliman, God always knows what he does. He made us different in order to make us suffer and to show us our impotence. Man to man, we have a very heartfelt relationship. Our friendship is sincere. It has come out of all our trials stronger than ever, but this time we can do nothing because the conflict is between our peoples, and we are powerless to alter the course of events. We are dragged along in the currents of history, and we have to suffer its whims. Every human being must follow the course of his destiny just as a drop of water flows with the current of a river. God alone knows the secrets of all these movements. To tell you the whole truth, I think we will join our son David in the Holy Land."

Sheik Sliman was quite shocked by this confession. "You astonish me very much, Rabbinas. Have you thought it out well? Zionism is a European movement, completely alien to you. It may be good for those without a country, the victims of pogroms and the survivors of concentration camps. But the Jews here have nothing in common with them. They have never been driven out of their homes. Centuries of peaceful coexistence cannot be wiped out by a few years of foreign propaganda. What will you do there? You will be like the Arabs here who are colonized by the French; your colonizers will be the Jews from Europe. They are more educated, longer in the country, hard-working, dynamic, and you will never match stride with them. It's madness, Rabbinas, to leave your homeland where everybody loves you and respects you, and to embark on some strange adventure. It may be good for the young, but at your age! May God give you reason!"

The insinuation was clear; accompanied by certain gestures, this Arabic formula meant in reality "You must have lost your mind." Rabbinas nodded his head as a sign of agreement and said, "I know all that, Sheik Sliman, but I don't know what is driving me towards this adventure, as you call it. The Holy Land is like a magnet that draws us to her by some magic power. For more than two thousand years, Jews from all over the world have repeated their vow of 'Next year in Jerusalem.' And now, it's no longer a dream but a reality. My friend, I wish you could understand me!"

For Rabbinas and his family, it would take nine years for their dream to become a reality. In 1957 he sold everything he owned at a bargain rate and left the country where, as he said, his fathers had lived for a thousand years. On the day before his departure all of the town dwellers, Jews and Arabs, came to wish him "Bon Voyage" and "Good Health." Sheik Sliman was among them. He couldn't stay for long because he had difficulty hiding his emotions.

"Rabbinas," he said, taking leave, "I hope that you will not have regrets, but if things turn out badly, don't forget that you always have a faithful friend here who will do everything to help you return to the country of your fathers."

"Sheik Sliman," replied Rabbinas, "I am leaving the land of my fathers for the land of my ancestors Abraham, Isaac, and Jacob. This privilege is not without its suffering. Come what may, I will not return here, but I will never forget our friendship. God give you long life!"

For the first and last time the two men embraced each other. On the next day, Rabbinas set sail for the Holy Land.

Chapter Nine

Mendel Weiss left the hospital and was immediately mustered out of the army for reasons of health. Besides, the war was drawing to a close. He took the morning bus and went back to the kibbutz. Gita was waiting for him in her room. As soon as he saw her, Mendel quickened his pace and hugged her very tightly. She was pallid and shook at his touch.

"How is Shlomit?" he asked. "Is there any decision?"

The response was vague. Both of them wanted to avoid calling things by their names; he, because he feared a shocking answer; she, because she had nothing encouraging to report. By tacit agreement, they kept quiet a moment. Then Mendel continued in a more direct tone.

"Did they find her parents?"

"No," his girl friend answered dryly.

Mendel heaved a sigh of relief. "So they haven't given up, have they? Are they going to stop looking for them?"

"Not yet. They're still awaiting an answer from the other side."

"Fine," said Mendel. "Nothing is lost yet, and we must not waste our time. If you agree, we will get married next week. There will be one less obstacle in our way; a good and warm home is a prerequisite for a legal adoption."

"Next week is fine with me," Gita said.

"Well," he said, "I'm going immediately to announce the news to Baruch, the kibbutz secretary, and try to see if they can hurry up the adoption procedure." He kissed her and left on the run.

Baruch was alone in his office. When he saw Mendel, he greeted him with a warm *Shalom*. "I'm happy that you got out of it okay," he said. "The kibbutz has already lost a dozen of its sons in this cursed war. How do you feel?"

"Fine, thanks," said Mendel. "Baruch, what news is there?"

"Oh, as usual. You work in the day and you're on guard at night. Oh yes, our citrus juice factory will be ready next month, and we are training the necessary manpower. Would you like to work there? It'll be a rest for you after what you've just gone through."

Mendel scarcely listened to him. "I wanted to talk to you about the child, about Shlomit. You know, Baruch, that we're thinking of adopting her, Gita and I. In order to make everything right, I came to tell you that we've decided to get married next week."

"*Mazel tov!*" said Baruch. "Unfortunately, I can't say anything about the adoption. It's a long and difficult matter. Of course, we'll do everything to help you. Patience, my friend, *Sav-la-nut*. As of now, I can only tell you what I told Gita last week, that we're waiting for an answer from the other side. It could take a week . . . or six months."

"Baruch, may I ask you to consider this matter very urgent and to give it your full attention?" begged Mendel.

"Certainly, I've already written three letters to the International Red Cross and will gladly send them a fourth next week. But, let's take a look at the mail first . . . Ah! Here is a letter with a Red Cross on the envelope. This could be it."

Baruch quickly opened the envelope. "It's written in French," he said. "It's no good reading it aloud to you. I will translate it when I've finished."

"Good," said Mendel nervously.

Baruch glanced over the letter with surprising speed. French was his native tongue. He was born in Belgium and he had lived there until the age of fifteen.

"You've won!" he said as he finished reading. "The Red

34

Cross has found the family after long hunting in a refugee camp near Jericho. The father, Amin Ibn-Hussein, cannot be traced. Salha, Amin's wife, is very sick and she has seven children to care for. They are all living in a tent on the meager food rations distributed by the U.N. They suffer a lot from the climate and often are hungry. Salha stated that it was enough to care for seven children, four of whom were not hers. She refused to take Jihada who isn't even her own daughter. She said that it was worth more for Jihada to live and be raised in a kibbutz where she would be able at least to eat her fill and have a bed to sleep in rather than suffer in a refugee camp. The poor woman signed a statement of her own free will, giving up all of her rights to Jihada and swearing never to lay claim to her."

A copy of the statement was attached to the letter. Baruch handed it over to Mendel who was shaking with emotion.

"The way is now clear for the adoption procedure," continued Baruch. "From now on, it's the Israeli authorities with whom you have to deal. Your marriage will certainly make their task easier. I will fix your file up tomorrow morning with copies of these letters and a hearty recommendation from the kibbutz. Good luck, Mendel, *Mazeltov!*"

"Thanks a lot, Baruch," stammered Mendel as he ran out to tell the good news to Gita.

The adoption procedure was not easy and short as Baruch and Mendel had believed. It lasted more than a year. One fine day, Mendel came home beaming. He had in his hand an identity booklet already opened to the page with the heading "Children." A name was written on it: "Shlomit." Mendel triumphantly pointed his finger to the name and yelled: "Shlomit! Shlomit Weiss, our daughter!" He and Gita hugged each other with emotion, and tears flowed down their cheeks.

They went right away to the nursery to see their daughter as if they wanted her to share in their joy. Shlomit was then sixteen months old. They found her naked from the waist up, bare-footed like all the children in the kibbutz. Only little white pants covered her, and a little cap protected her head from the sun. She was having fun in the sandbox with children her own age. On seeing them, she raised her head and squinted back at them.

"How beautiful she is!" Gita exclaimed. "Those beautiful dark eyes, those pink cheeks, and that cute little mouth!"

Mendel lifted her into his arms, hugged, and kissed her: "My daughter, my sweet daughter! Today, we will take her to our room, and this time, as her le-gal parents."

The day she became six years old, after a nice birthday party, Shlomit walked into her parents' room, crying. "Is it true?" she asked.

"What? What's the matter?" wondered Gita.

"Is it true that you are not my real parents? That's what Uzi just told me."

"Oh no," said Mendel angrily. "You don't have to listen to what they tell you. Of course you are our daughter, and we are your real parents." He patted her on the shoulder and put a chocolate bar in her mouth. "Go, sweetie. Go back to your swing," he said.

The child smiled, reassured. As soon as she left, Gita was unable to contain herself. "That was inevitable. You can't muzzle everybody. My sterility is no secret, and the whole kibbutz has followed this adoption story with interest. What we're doing is stupid and even dangerous for our daughter. I've always asked you to get the child ready for it little by little in order to avoid the big shock in the future. But you, with your hard-headedness, you're always set against my proposal."

Mendel was very bothered but didn't want to admit his mistake. "Yes," he said, "I've always rejected your suggestions precisely in order to spare her suffering. What? Do you want me to tell her that her parents are Arabs? Maybe, at an older age she would be more ready to accept the truth and understand that we had saved her life and prepared her for a better future."

"Your reasoning might be correct" retorted Gita, "if we were living alone in this world, but here nothing is a secret and what I fear most is that she will learn about her past from strangers, and this will be much worse. There is no need to tell her the whole story. We can simply inform her, in a gentle manner, that we have adopted her because she had no parents."

"And then someone else will tell her the rest," snarled Mendel. "No, thank you. I will never do that. She must be kept in the dark about her parentage. Furthermore, I've made up my mind: we will leave this kibbutz as soon as possible. I will look for a job in the city where we will be completely unknown."

"What?" Gita cried out. "What can you do in the city? You know very well that we will leave the kibbutz empty-handed. We own nothing. I no longer have the strength to begin life all over again. Think of me, Mendel! Think of Shlomit!"

"It's precisely because of her that we must leave," he answered with a commanding tone.

"Oh, Mendel, you do everything on the spur of the moment, and everybody has to follow your whim. First, the idea of adoption. Then, your stupid decision to keep it a secret, which is beginning to eat at my insides. And now, another folly: throwing everything in the air, leaving a secure and peaceful life in the kibbutz for some unknown venture as if we were still twenty years old. Really, I don't understand, Mendel. Why do you enjoy making us suffer?"

"I adopted her because of you," Mendel cut in, alluding to his wife's inability to bear children.'

"You are cruel!" she cried and walked out of the room.

It was in Tel Aviv that Shlomit Weiss began her elementary education. Thanks to Baruch's recommendation, Mendel had easily found work there. The burgeoning administration of the new state needed staff, and although Mendel Weiss was not endowed with a special talent, he was hired as a comptroller's assistant in the Ministry of Finance. Mendel was not hard to get along with. He took any kind of job because from that moment on, he had one goal in life: to provide his daughter with the best possible education. He rented an apartment in one of the finest residential sections of the city to make it possible for her to attend the best school in town. The rent was quite beyond his rather modest income, but he was able to make do by economizing in other areas.

Shlomit loved school. She brought home good grades and her progress was obvious. On his part, Mendel was eager to succeed in his work. He took two advanced courses and went up the ladder after each one. His pay improved and he was entrusted with more important jobs in the Ministry. Gita stayed home during the first five years in Tel Aviv because she wanted to be completely available to Shlomit who needed her care and affection.

In the sixth year they began to consider the possibility of enrolling Shlomit in the prestigious private school in Tel Aviv. This entailed rather high tuition fees, an entirely new expense unknown in elementary school where education was free. Most of her classmates had already applied, and time was running short. Mendel and Gita worked and reworked their budget figures. They surely could not compete with the *nouveaux riches* in the district who didn't have to count their expenses. After a careful consideration of the matter, they decided to send Shlomit to high school. Gita would work to pay for her secondary education.

Shlomit had a flawless record during her six years of secondary education. The sacrifice had not been in vain. Her grades were excellent. She was also an outstanding friend, sincere and devoted to her schoolmates. For many consecutive years, she was elected and re-elected head of her student government. She became a scout leader, and she distinguished herself in *Gadna* courses, the mandatory paramilitary training for boys and girls between the ages of fifteen and eighteen. In them she showed zealousness and unbounded patriotism. She even completed an arduous course that qualified her to instruct her underclassmen. When tension mounted at the borders and farming villages were shelled by the Syrians well entrenched on the Golan heights, she was always among the first to organize relief for the victims whom she frequently visited. When she returned, her vivid descriptions of what she had seen and her patriotic fervor would arouse the enthusiasm of her classmates. Three times, she went with all of her class to live and work for two weeks on the Syrian border, in a kibbutz her school had adopted, rebuilding what the Syrian shells had destroyed and helping in the fields. Such powerful bonds were created between her class and the kibbutz that she decided, along with her group, to settle there after her military service. She believed that was the greatest service she could render to her besieged country.

June 1966 came in leaps and bounds. It was the month of the terrifying baccalaureate examinations. Shlomit had just celebrated her eighteenth birthday. She was more beautiful than ever. Her brown oval face with its round chin and fine pink lips was always lit with a smile that showed her white regular teeth. Her dark shiny eyes on a spotless white background made her schoolmates and neighborhood acquaintances marvel. And her direct, penetrating gaze expressed intelligence and perspicacity. Her well-proportioned body and firm bust added to her attractiveness. Her black hair was silken, cut short, and curled.

Up to that time, she had had no romantic adventures. Innocent flirtation without consequence was her entire experience. She tactfully rebuffed, with a smile on her face, a large number of boys who seemed rather eager to seduce her. They knew that she was unavailable, and she was often teased about it. "There's no hurry," she would answer. "Everything will happen in time. The human being is not an animal. Women, particularly, must be in love before surrendering to physical temptations. I myself have not yet known this kind of love."

"While you are waiting, let me admire you, beautiful brunette," her best boy friend would sigh. "Let me look at you if I can't touch you. Let me feel close to you if I can't hug you."

Shlomit was very friendly, but her schoolmates didn't arouse in her any sexual desire. "They're like my brothers," she would say. "We are together almost ten hours a day, in the morning at school, in the evening in our youth club. We know each other too well." She sought the mysterious, the far-off, the exotic. A verse from Baudelaire had fascinated her: "Hell or heaven, who cares as long as one can plunge into the unknown in order to find the new." What was known, what was within reach, bored her. She dreamed of getting away from it all and of diving into the unfathomable depths in search of excitement.

After eleven years of civil service, Mendel was promoted to a very high rank in the Finance Ministry. He had very good connections with the incumbent party leaders and was the protégé of the finance minister himself. Both were native of the same Eastern European village. The minister had known Mendel's father very well and was very saddened by his tragic disappearance in Auschwitz. Mendel was of great service to the party during the campaign. He had no political ambition of his own, and this allowed him to devote himself to the political promotion of his benefactors. It was his way of thanking them and also of safeguarding his position and his privileges in the Ministry.

In this very politicized little country, political power was the touchstone to everything. In the incumbent party, the small group of men who wielded real power made and unmade ministers and representatives, mayors and high officials, and dispensed at will whole slices of the national pie. It was this party that had created millionaires, the new class of *nouveaux riches* on the north side of Tel Aviv, and that had at the same time been responsible for the wretchedness and the stripping of newly arrived immigrants from Asia and Africa, who had no access to the pie made in Europe. All of this, of course, was done in conformity with the democratic rules, which went to the drumbeat of elections and according to the law of the majority. The party bosses did everything to increase their membership at the grass-roots level, but the oligarchy in power allowed no intruders at the top.

Mendel's job was to enroll in the party these "Oriental" newcomers, as they were called in the current political jargon.

His job was quite easy. He didn't have to get them embroiled in political and partisan complications or ideological struggles; that would have been a waste of time. He only had to persuade them to vote for the party. To this end all means were good. The best technique was to find in the mass of people clever and pushy rabble-rousers to whom would be given anything, as one regional secretary said to Mendel, from a glass of brandy to an apartment. These election mercenaries were hired for a few months up to election day. After the voting, they vanished. "For four years," the saying went, "the voters speak to the walls which don't hear their voices, and once every four years, during parliamentary elections, the walls speak to them through giant posters, microphones and amplifiers and ask for their voices, that is, for their votes."

For three months, Mendel was on leave from his Ministry office. He was at party headquarters from which he organized the election strategy, leaving tactics to his agents who came to him every day to report on their progress. He often had to settle violent arguments between his agents. One day, after one of his inspection trips, he came home disgusted at these human animals. "They are like Arabs, Gita. They are dirty; they eat with their hands sitting on a mat; they don't like to work. The only thing they know is to make a child every year with their enslaved and backward women."

Gita answered him calmly: "Mendel, how can you say these things? It's true that they have taken on the ways of the countries in which they had lived,"—she carefully avoided, with good reason, mentioning the word *Arabs*—"but they are our brothers. We will educate them. We will civilize them. Maybe not the parents but the children, for sure. Don't forget that these children will be soldiers and will defend our country against its enemies. Even today, the army is made up of sixty percent Orientals, and you can't put them down as you're doing. You . . ."

"You know nothing, you see nothing," Mendel angrily interrupted. "Since I began working on these elections, I have been looking and learning. Do you realize what is going on? One of those patriarchs, a clan leader, asked us the other day

41

to get him a license to sell fruits. He swore on the Bible to get us fifty-six votes. Another with thirty-four votes in his pocket even dared to ask us for a television set. They want luxury now. They naively believe that they are asking for their share of the gifts sent by American Jews. And you mean to tell me that these people deserve democracy? They've never voted in their lives!"

"And what did you tell them?" Gita asked with irony.

"The first one will have his license, which will cost us nothing. The second will get a loan, which will cover in part his son's work for the party in the election campaign. What can you do? If we don't do that, other parties will, and we've got to win these elections. My future at the Ministry is at stake, as you well know."

Gita wanted to reply that there was no difference between him and them, but she feared one of his outbreaks of anger which had become more and more frequent. She threw out a general, less-pointed response: "Yes, you know what our wise fathers said: 'It isn't the mouse which is the thief; it's the hole that lures him.' "

Mendel avoided this kind of argument in front of his daughter. If, by chance, she appeared unexpectedly in the middle of one of these heated discussions, he would stop immediately without even finishing his sentence or would shift to Yiddish. This ploy irked the young girl. One day, exasperated, she said to him: "Dad, you should have the courage of your convictions. What are you always hiding from me? Am I a stranger to you?"

As for the Yiddish language, she hated it as did all of her generation for whom Hebrew was the native tongue. Yiddish reminded them of a history of humiliation, of expulsions, pogroms, and persecutions. And of a servile and miserable Jewish existence in the Diaspora. Sometimes, they hurled invectives at their parents, even breaking their hearts with the accusation that the six million were led into crematorial ovens without resisting, without fighting. Shlomit carefully avoided alluding to this cruel and certainly unprovable accusation in front of her father, who himself had escaped from Auschwitz, where his whole family had been massacred. But she didn't hide from her family her aversion for that language and she doggedly refused to learn it or even listen to it. "If we have to learn another language," she flatly said during the same discussion, "it should rather be Arabic, which would allow us to communicate with our neighbors when peace comes, and even with our brothers from Arab countries who return everyday to Zion with no knowledge of Hebrew."

This statement had a disastrous effect on her father. Fate seemed set against him. All his efforts to isolate his daughter from the Oriental world of her forebears had precisely the opposite effect: pushing her closer to it. 'Why then all these sacrifices?' he thought. He could have lived in a very inexpensive section of Tel Aviv where his daughter would have come into direct contact with this Judeo-Arab world. Maybe then, reality would have turned her off. But here, in this school, an almost exclusively European one, his daughter's professors, among the most liberal in the country, didn't conceal their discontent with the political setup and their displeasure at the discriminatory situation whose victims were immigrants from Arab countries. Some of them even dared to talk about discrimination against Arabs.

Putting an end to his bitter thoughts, Mendel, this time, decided on a frontal attack: "Arabic!?" he yelled. "Oh, no! This country must preserve its European nature. Otherwise, it will perish. Since we can't do without this Oriental-Arab immigration, we must, at all costs, westernize these people. If we fail to do so, the country will sink into the backward ways of Levantinism which will make us no different from our neighbors. The Arab language is a basic element of this Levantinization. Why not take Islam while we're at it?"

"What you are saying is racism!" cried Shlomit, obviously irritated. "Have you become a racist, you who have suffered from the most horrible of racisms?"

"No, Shlomit," answered her father. "This is not racism. It's a question of instinct, survival instinct, a question of national security. Up to now, we have won out over our enemies, thanks

43

to our quality, not to our quantity. This quality must always prevail. This is why the European hegemony is a political imperative. Today, Jews from the West and the United States are free to emigrate to Israel, but they don't seem to want to. Jews from Russia want to emigrate, but they are not allowed to. The sole reservoir of potential immigrants is in Arab countries, in Africa and in Asia. We don't have a choice because we need them. But as I said before, we must europeanize them."

"You mean we must cut out their tongues, force them to forget their native languages and maybe make them learn Yiddish," replied Shlomit sarcastically.

"Not necessarily," Mendel assured her. "The school and the army have done an excellent job without making them learn Yiddish."

"But the school and the army are good for children and young people, not for their parents who also have a personality and a dignity. They are happy as they are and they don't want to live disguised all their lives, and wear a Western mask. And by what right would you presume to transform them?"

"They must get in step with the Western world if they don't want to miss the boat. This is the twentieth century. All civilized countries are running to keep up with progress. In this country, we must gallop; there's no room for laggards—to hell with them!"

Enraged, Shlomit decided to counterattack in terms that would certainly provoke her father's ire: "You know what the Arab proverb says about speed, don't you? It says that speed is the work of the devil. Whether you like it or not, we are in the Middle East, in the Arab Middle East—the Levant, as you call it—and we cannot remain indefinitely European, particularly if we are seriously thinking about peace with our neighbors. Besides, that is one of the main points of their propaganda, and I think there is a certain truth to it. They say that we are a foreign element in this region, and what they are afraid of is precisely that speed about which you are boasting. It is your generation that talks this way. The young *Sabras* don't necessarily share your point of view. The difference between your generation and ours isn't only political, it's also physical. You

44

only have to compare our young people to their parents and the difference hits you in the eye. They're taller, better built, darker. I, for example, do I look like you? Not at all. You're blond with gray eyes; my mother is pale in complexion with freckles. And look at me! I am brown with dark eyes, a real native of this country. My friends often tease me about it: 'You don't look at all like your parents,' they say. 'Maybe you're the milkman's daughter.' Or better still: 'Where did your parents buy you? How much did you cost them?' "

Mendel sharply raised his head and turned towards his wife who had kept silent through this long conversation. Their gazes met. In their eyes were surprise and shock. Mendel tried to say something; his mouth remained open but uttered not a sound. His tongue stuck to his palate. Gita, always apprehensive of a mishap, came to his rescue: "Go to your room, my child. You must be tired, you certainly have homework to do."

Shlomit kissed her on the cheek and bade her good night.

Alone with her husband, Gita couldn't hold her tears in check. Turning to him, she said begrudgingly: "What a fine job you've done, Mendel. Now look at the mess we've gotten ourselves in. I didn't dare open my mouth during the whole conversation, but I'm not going to stifle myself any more. I agree with her, and it seems to me that you have become a racist. You are no longer the Mendel I knew at the kibbutz. Is it your success at the Ministry that has gone to your head? Or is it politics which has transformed you and corrupted you? Why smash the idealistic drive in this poor girl? Let her lead her life as she understands it. Let her discover for herself the evils of this society. From the day you brought her to me, seventeen years ago, I've never stopped fearing for her. When will she learn the truth about her parentage? Her last statement is gnawing at me. Do you think she knows? Or was it just plain coincidence? I was so close to telling her that we had not bought her but adopted her. I don't know what held me back. Maybe your eyes, your tearful and fearful look. Your mouth stayed open and dumb. I can't take any more of it, Mendel. You're going to kill me."

In his reply, Mendel seemed remorseful: "I'm sorry, Gita. Forgive me for making you suffer for my whims. You've come a long way with me, and maybe we shouldn't have . . . I felt my insides withering. I felt dizzy, everything around me was spinning. My eyes were open, but I couldn't see anything. An unbearable buzz was in my ears. I almost passed out. This scene should never happen again. I'm beginning to think that adoption is a dangerous thing, or maybe the child should bear some resemblance, some physical . . ."

"No!" Gita interrupted, losing her patience. "It is not the adoption which is dangerous. Hiding the truth from the child, that's where the danger lies. It can lead to very serious consequences. I've already told you that over and over again, but you . . ." She couldn't finish her sentence. Choked with tears, she left the room. Mendel followed her, muttering some words of consolation, but she angrily slammed the door in his face.

Chapter Ten

The boat dropped anchor in Haifa six hours late. Tourists came ashore first. North African immigrants were in the hold below deck. It took the first of them four hours to get down the gangplank. On shore, there was a tremendous hustle and bustle. Relatives had come from all over the country to welcome the new immigrants, the *Olim*. They were seen scurrying from office to office to get information on the time and place of arrival. Some of them had telegrams in their hands, but the information they contained was in sharp conflict with the facts. The incessant and frenzied going and coming made the waiting room look like a country fair.

David Levy had been waiting since eight o'clock that morning, the scheduled time of arrival. It was now two o'clock in the afternoon, but David had kept his cool. What's important, he thought, is that they get here safe and sound. Since his discharge from the army, David had been living in Hadera where he rented an apartment. Thanks to his knowledge of Hebrew, learned in Tunisia, and thanks to his broad education, he had succeeded in getting a quite responsible job in the foreign exchange department of a large bank in town. Very thrifty, he had set aside a little money to help his family over the rough spots in the first stage of their immigration. He was aware of the major difficulties that North African families faced as soon as they arrived in the new country. He could take over the money problems, he thought, but he was very apprehensive about the reaction his father would have to the psychological

47

and social obstacles against which he himself could do nothing. He took small comfort in the fact that he hadn't persuaded his parents to emigrate. Each time they had asked his advice, he replied that it was their own decision and that he would do all that he could to help them adjust. He also knew that some of his friends who had taken the same precautions could not escape their parents' recriminations. They don't have any choice, he concluded. Life in an Arab country is no longer possible for Jews. It's an historical development which is beyond our control and to which we must submit.

The loudspeaker announced that immigrants were beginning to land, and could be seen from behind the fence. David felt his heart beat quicker. It was almost nine years since he had last seen his father, his mother and his brother Rahamim, born while he was away in the forced labor camp as a prisoner of the Germans. He was particularly anxious to see the youngest in the family, his sister Rachel, whom he didn't know. David couldn't take his eyes off the gangplank.

Some immigrants were already on shore. They were dressed in Arab garb. They wore huge leather slippers on their feet, and large robes covered them from head to toe. All the men were dressed in the same way; only by the color of their beards could one tell them apart, black for the young, white for the old. They were Moroccan Jews, mountain people from the Atlas. David had never seen such Jews. He came closer to the fence to have a better look.

"They are my relatives," declared the young man standing next to him, who seemed aware of David's curiosity.

"But you!" David stammered, surprised to see his neighbor dressed impeccably as a European, close-shaven, his eyes shielded by strikingly smart sunglasses.

The elegant Moroccan replied, "Oh, they're excellent farmers; the country needs them. They are very simple, pious Jews, happy with the little they have. They will be sent to development areas where they're going to build farming villages to feed the population. Don't worry about their beards and their robes; their children . . ."

"See you later," interrupted David. "Here are my folks."

Rabbinas came down the gangway at a quick step. His wife Esther followed him holding Rachel by the hand, and behind her walked Rahamim carrying a suitcase. A couple of Europeans were ahead of them. The European man was the first to set foot on shore; he held his hand out to Rabbinas to assist him. The old man almost fell, stumbling on the last step of the gangway. Rahamim grabbed his father and prevented the accident. Rabbinas paid it no mind; he bent down, squatted, and threw himself on the ground, his face on the burning asphalt. He fanatically kissed the Holy Land and got up, tears in his eyes, his lips quivering. Then he intoned in his stentorian voice the prayer of *Shehehiyanu*, raising his hands to Heaven to thank his creator for letting him live long enough to see this blessed moment.

Everything stopped. The immigrants stood still on the gangplank. Relatives who were waiting for the newcomers seemed frozen as if by enchantment. Even the Jewish Agency employees for whom this was not a new sight left their offices to witness the spectacle. "They have faith, these people," said one of them to his friends. "The faith which moves mountains. We, too, need it."

David watched the scene with strong emotions. He wanted to jump over the fence, but the guard prevented him. A few moments later, he headed to the waiting room where his family had gone. After warm hugging and kissing with the whole family, his father gave him the traditional blessing and introduced him to the European couple with whom they had struck up a friendship during the six-day crossing.

"On the boat, we met Mr. and Mrs. Bienstock," Rabbinas told his son. Addressing the couple, he added: "This is David, my son I told you about."

David shook their hands and muttered a polite Hebrew greeting. "Shalom!" Mr. Bienstock answered him. "You have a father to treasure, David. It was a great honor for us to meet him. We have been able to have a conversation thanks to the little Hebrew I know. We have discovered a truly Jewish heart,

49

a universal mind and a fount of knowledge. You must cherish him and surround him with care. He is a benediction for Israel."

"Oh, let's not exaggerate," Rabbinas said, humbly. He told David how his friend had tried to talk to him in a Jewish language he didn't even know existed. "They call it Yiddish," he explained, "and Mr. Bienstock showed me a newspaper written in this language. The letters were really in Hebrew, but I couldn't understand a thing." David listened patiently to his father who continued: "Mr. Bienstock was amazed, very amazed. He was sure that all Jews knew this language. I showed him my poems, also written in Hebrew letters, but he couldn't read the first word because the language was Arabic." Obviously satisfied with his own story, the old man concluded: "We realized that it was the *galuth*, the exile, which had separated us, and that each Jewish community had borrowed the language of the country in which it was in exile. Today we return to Zion and to our national language, Hebrew."

"Yes, Rabbinas!" said Bienstock, "One country, one people, one language!"

He hadn't finished his statement when a strong voice announced over the loudspeaker: "Mr. and Mrs. Bienstock, the Pinsky family, and Lea Berkowitz, please report to office number nine. I repeat, Mr. and Mrs. Bienstock . . ."

"Oh, they're calling us," said Bienstock. "We must leave you, Mr. Levy. We will certainly come to see you soon. Send me your address as soon as you are settled. Here is the address of my brother in Tel Aviv."

"But what?" said Rabbinas, visibly surprised. "You're leaving us? They told us that we would be together."

"I really don't understand," answered Bienstock. "We'd better go now. Good-bye, Rabbinas. Shalom to all of you!"

The loudspeaker repeated its announcement, and Bienstock hastened off to office number nine, followed by his wife.

The line was rather long. The immigrants and their relatives waited to get through the formalities. They were told that they would be sent to a new village of North African immigrants down south. Only two offices were open to them, numbers three and five. At this slow step, David thought, two hours wouldn't be enough. He walked along the dock and saw only North Africans; a mixture of French and Arabic wafted up from this noisy line. He heard endless complaints. Already! he wondered. Babies cried and added to the hubbub. He came close to a group which seemed to be very unhappy. The more articulate among them told him that they had been stacked up in the hold in suffocating heat, whole families together without any privacy, and that in order to breathe they had to go up on deck. They lamented about the food which was tasteless and inedible, and about the service which completely ignored them. "In one word," said one immigrant, "we were treated like animals."

David went back to his father and asked: "Tell me, father, how was the voyage? How did you feel in the boat?"

"Thank God," answered his father. "We don't have to complain."

"But down there they're saying . . ."

"You know your father," interrupted Mrs. Levy; "he never complains. He would say, 'Thank God; it could have been worse; we could have drowned.' Oh, no! I must tell you, my son. Everything you heard is true. What penance we endured! It was the worst week in my life."

"Esther, enough of that, please; everything is over and done with," said her husband. "*Eretz-Israel* is reached through suffering. We must come here purified, and the suffering has cleansed us."

David did not seem satisfied with this reply. Nine years of living in Israel had sharpened his sense of justice, and in his inmost heart, he scorned his father's resignation. Turning to him, he asked bluntly: "Tell me, Dad: Mr. Bienstock, was he down in the hold with you?"

"No, my son, but I met him everyday on the deck. Why?"

David spent a few minutes in small talk and then excused himself, saying he would be right back. Something bothered him; he wanted to clear his mind of doubts. He went back to office number nine. There were no lines. Three employees were peacefully drinking tea. He approached the first and asked in flawless Hebrew: "Please excuse me; has Mr. Bienstock been through here?"

The man glanced at his list. "Yes," he said, "he has been housed somewhere near Tel Aviv. He has a brother there."

"But how can that be?" questioned David. "He came on the same boat as those people over there who are waiting to be sent down south to a new village. Why were they separated?"

The three men burst out laughing. The question was very naive, and they didn't expect it. One of them answered: "But you should know that there are two kinds of immigration, Western immigration such as Mr. Bienstock's, and Oriental immigration like the North Africans and other people from Arab countries. As soon as they get here, the Oriental immigrants are forwarded to development areas according to the slogan 'From boat to farm'. These peddlers and craftsmen must be transformed into farmers rooted in their soil. For the Western immigrants, that's another story. They are city folk, professionals, educated. Even the workers among them are specialists. They also have relatives here and organizations of well-established people from their countries of origin that help them take roots in this country. They're sent to metropolitan areas. There, they'll study Hebrew for five months and have time to shop around for a job. They're given free board and room. Some are even put up in hotels. You see, we didn't get that chance when we came. They didn't spoil us this way. I've been around for fifteen years. There was nothing for us. What about you? Were you born here?"

"No!" replied David, irritated. "I'm an Oriental, as you call it. I volunteered from Tunisia in 1948 to fight for the country. They didn't give me anything either." Then he burst out in sarcastic laughter. "Funny! Very funny! People from Eastern Europe are now the 'Westerners' and those from the *Maghreb*, the *maarav*, the West, are called 'Orientals.' Don't you know your geography, or maybe this discrimination isn't geographic, is it?"

"No, sir. It isn't geographic. It's human, sir, human."

"Inhuman, you mean!" yelled David, angered and disappointed. Then he returned to his family.

The Levy family's turn came. While David was filling out the forms, the clerk asked the family to move a bit to the right. A nurse in white stood there, holding a perforated can in her hand. Nobody took the trouble to explain what was happening. David stopped the family from going on.

"What's with this box?" he asked the nurse.

"DDT," answered the young woman. "It's for lice; it's to prevent an epidemic."

"What?" yelled David. "But you can see quite well that they're clean. No, you will not do that. That's humiliating, and phony."

The young woman waited for her orders. A man came and explained to David the importance of DDT, that it was for the good of the family and the public health.

"And Bienstock?" David asked. "Did you powder his head with DDT?"

"I don't know whom you are talking about, but judging from the name, Bienstock comes from Europe; it's not the same thing. These people come from North Africa. They lived there in caves without the most elementary hygiene. They may be carrying parasites."

David was dumfounded. "My family, living in caves? Where did you get this nonsense?" Such ignorance seemed monstrous to him, and he stopped cold, turned red and wiped the sweat off his forehead. "Not a speck! No DDT, I tell you, even if they have to stay here forever!," he yelled.

Finally, the Levy family was allowed to leave without a DDT treatment. "Your family is really clean, sir," said the man in charge. "But they're an exception. I wish you good luck."

The truck carrying five families got to its destination very late that night. It was very dark when the immigrants climbed down. Someone came and gave the head of each family a key to his apartment. David took his family's key and went ahead to open the door. A small table stood at the entry hall, with a kerosene lamp and matches. David struck a match and lit the brand-new wick. A light wisp of smoke rose up. The flame flickered a few seconds. Then he put the shade on the lamp, and the flame leveled off allowing them to see the inside of their new dwelling place.

The apartment was brand-new. Temporary curtains were hung over the windows, which were still missing. There were two little rooms, a kitchenette, a shower, and a balcony. A white table and four stools took up the middle of the apartment. In the kitchen there was a kerosene stove, a can of fuel, two loaves of bread, eggs, vegetables, cans of food, fruit, and other staples—enough food for two or three days.

Everybody was exhausted. No one felt like eating. The mother shared her bed with the little girl and got the three others ready for her husband and two sons. Then she put out the light and the family went to sleep.

Rabbinas was the first to awaken. He quietly washed up, then put on his *talith* and *tefillin* and began his morning prayer. "God forgive me," he said, "for praying alone and not with a *minyan*, but I don't know where we are. I don't even know if there are people living here or if there is a synagogue."

His wife got up soon afterward, then David and the other children. After a hasty breakfast, Rabbinas went out with his two sons to get acquainted with the village folk. The office was nearby. They discovered that there were already two hundred families in the village, Jews from Morocco, Tunisia, and Libya. They were shown the school, the general store, and other small apartments like theirs, which already occupied. Rabbinas was told to enroll his two children in the school that very day. As far as he was concerned, he would do well to sign up for work which he could get in two or three days.

"What work?" David asked.

"Planting trees," answered the clerk. "Trees help to fix the sandy soil and also to provide shade. As you can see, it's very hot here. Your father will dig holes. It's a little hard in the beginning, but he'll get used to it."

Rabbinas understood most of what was said. "We will see," he told the clerk. "I will come back next week." He took the hand of his oldest son whose embarrassment he understood. "David, my boy," he said, "don't worry. You must know that I brought some money with me from the sale of the store and the house. We will be able to hold out for a while, and in the meantime I'll keep my eyes open to see what I can do. Maybe a little shop to keep me busy and to take care of some of the family's needs."

"Father," said David, "you must not spend anything of what you brought with you. You should put all the money in the bank. Meanwhile, I'll give you what you need."

"No, David," his father answered, "I hope I'll never need your help. I've worked hard all my life. I'll give you all the money I have; please do as you said. If I need anything, I'll write to you."

"As you wish, Father," said David respectfully.

"Thank you for coming here and helping us. You should go back to your job now. God protect you." He placed his two hands on his son's head and blessed him. With tears in his eyes, David kissed his father's hands. It was the custom in the Rabbinas family.

David kissed his mother and sister, then turned to his brother: "Rahamim, you have only one obligation: to study and succeed, as you've always done. I will help you with all that I've got."

"Thank you, David. I will do my best," his young brother assured him.

On taking leave, David promised his mother to come every Friday and spend the Sabbath with the family.

Rahamim was fourteen years old when he was introduced to the principal of the village school. He felt very much like a foreigner. He had to speak a new language, make new friends, live in inhuman surroundings which disgusted him at first sight. His mother had gotten together a little file containing all his report cards and his many honor certificates from the French school in his hometown; it was a testimony to his scholarly brilliance. He had been promoted to the third year of high school when his father's decision to go to Israel was made known. He had a very good grasp of French; he had already studied English for two years; and he excelled in math and science. 'Am I going to lose my head start because of the change?' he wondered with a lot of apprehension. He spoke Hebrew with difficulty but he could read and write this language pretty well. He managed to answer the principal's questions about his previous studies. The principal was amazed to discover the high level of this teen-ager's learning.

"Hebrew will be your only problem," he said, "and only temporarily. I'm sure you will catch up very quickly. For the rest, you are well ahead of students of your age who are in the eighth grade. Since we're toward the end of the school year, I advise you to take seventh-year courses so as to improve your Hebrew and, come September, you will be in the eighth grade, which is, in fact, the final year for the school and for the village as a whole."

Then the principal took him to the seventh-grade class-room. He opened the door and introduced him to the teacher, Elana, and to the students.

"This is a new student," he said. "His name is Rahamim Levy; he is a new immigrant." Some students began to laugh; others eyed him from head to toe. Rahamim was very embarrassed in his new suit and shiny shoes, which clashed with the shabby old clothes of his new classmates and with their rubber shoes. His appearance was impeccable, his hair very carefully combed. The teacher welcomed him and showed him to his seat. He sat down immediately and had to face off the stares of his classmates.

As soon as the principal left the room, chaos broke loose. Students left their seats without asking permission of their teacher, marched around the new student, and assailed him with questions.

"Where do you come from? Are you the son of a prince?" inquired one of them.

"Where did you get that suit?" asked another, feeling the cloth between his fingers.

"And those shoes!" exclaimed a third, hitting them with his fist. "Hey, you have a little money to give us? If you're so rich, what are you doing here? You are not a *voosvoos*, are you? You're not Yiddish!"

The teacher tried to hush them up but to no avail. The bell saved Rahamim. The group went out pell-mell from the classroom to the playground. Rahamim held back his tears, but he felt a crushing weight in his chest which prevented him from breathing. "What have they got against me?" he stammered. Elana, who had stayed behind for the sole purpose of comforting him, answered: "They are not malicious; they are simply curious like everyone else, and very poor."

"Like everyone else?" asked Rahamim.

"Almost everybody in this village. There are many large families here with very, very low income, scarcely enough to feed their children. The noonday meal is served at the school, free for all. The students are North African immigrants like you." Very embarrassed, she added, "Rahamim, you look like a very bright boy to me. Please be patient with them. You'll see that they'll like you a lot. Maybe it would be better if you dressed a little more plainly, somewhat like them."

"Everything I have is brand-new," answered Rahamim. "I'll have to tell my mother to buy me some clothes from here," he said.

"Thanks for your understanding," said Elana. "Besides, I've got to visit you some day and welcome your whole family."

Rahamim went back home and didn't return to school that day. He told his mother about his misadventure. She took him to the village store and, on their return, Rahamim was dressed like his classmates—in cheap clothing.

The next day, he made a less spectacular entrance in the

class and didn't cause a ripple. He had already been adopted and accepted by his classmates, he thought. But at the end of his second day, he began to doubt if the acceptance was mutual. He was amazed at the low level of scholarship and particularly at the lack of discipline. Elana made exhausting efforts to calm down these devils who never stopped chatting, yelling, getting out of their seats, and interrupting. She was very young and inexperienced. She was, in fact, a nineteen-year-old soldier who was doing her time, like many of her female fellows-in-arms, teaching in a village of immigrants.

The arithmetic exercises were childish. They were still doing multiplication and division, and even at that low level, his classmates didn't seem to understand. Elana had to repeat the same exercise many times. Rahamim nostalgically remembered his algebra and geometry problems. What was most striking to him was the absolute ignorance of these students in Hebrew and in the reading of Biblical texts. They couldn't even read without stumbling. When it was his turn to read, Elana wanted to pass him by, but Rahamim latched on very quickly after the youngster ahead of him, and his teacher let him go on, pleasantly surprised. His reading flowed without a stop or error. When he finished the paragraph, she couldn't help but congratulate him in front of the whole class. His classmates were stupefied, unable to understand this reading magic on the part of this new student.

It was only when she visited the Levy family that Elana could solve the riddle. She found her chat with Rabbinas very revealing and very instructive. Her visits to the Levys became more frequent. There, she told her colleagues, was her compensation for the tough and thankless days of work at the school.

Three weeks had slipped by since the Levy family's arrival at the village. Rabbinas hadn't worked a single day. With trepidation he saw his savings melt away with a speed unmatched in his own country. He had miscalculated. At this rate he realized he would wipe out everything in six months instead of three years as he had originally anticipated.

"I must try the job they offered me," he said to his wife.

"You? At your age?" she objected. "You are already past sixty. After your store and your position, and the respect that everybody gave you over there, Jews and Arabs!"

"Please, Esther dear, let's not talk about the past. It is dead and buried. Let's think about the present. I can't stay idle. I'll go mad. I will try this job for two or three days next week."

"Try it out if you like," replied his wife unconvinced.

On the next day, at six o'clock in the morning, Rabbinas was among the workers waiting for the truck that would take them to work. After they got to the labor site, he was given a pick and a shovel, and one of the men named Dahan instructed him on the use of these tools. Rabbinas had never in his life touched such tools. "Back at home, that was Arab's work," he said to his teacher.

"The same with us," answered Dahan, "I am from Casablanca where I was a tailor, a master cutter. I looked all around for work in my line, but everything is dead here. I heard that in Tel Aviv I might find something, but how can I get there? Who would take care of my wife and five children?"

Rabbinas began to forget his problems and to feel empathy for the other man. "Are you used to this kind of work? Do you earn enough to support your family?" he asked, obviously concerned.

"No to both questions," Dahan replied. "I do it because I have no choice. Thank God, I'm still young and strong. But . . . you? This is no job for you . . . As for the pay, it isn't normal worker's wages. They call it *dahak*. They even explained to me that it was some kind of disguised charity. We are given a ridiculous daily pittance, enough to buy bread and vegetables. To make ends meet, my wife, I'm ashamed to admit, rounds out our budget by doing housework for a *voosvoos* family, three miles from the village. My wife, who had a maid in Casablanca!"

Rabbinas was very upset by this confession. He tried to drive out of his mind an analogy which kept returning. "Great

59

God," he sighed. "No, my Lord, don't sink me that low. I'd rather die." Then, he walked over to the patch of land that Dahan showed him, seized his pick and began to strike. The result was almost nil, but there was nobody there to supervise his work. "Disguised charity," he said. "What a shame! All my life, I have been the one to give charity."

After the first hour of work, he was exhausted. His back ached, his pulse was racing, he was panting and sweating, and his knees were shaking. He stopped a moment and then started again at his job. "No charity," he decided, "I don't want anything for nothing."

But all his efforts were in vain. At the end of the second hour, he passed out, and Dahan had to call an ambulance which took him away unconscious.

Mrs. Levy was scared out of her wits. "I told him it wasn't his kind of work. A man past sixty who has never done any physical work in his life! But he wouldn't listen to me." His daughter was in tears. Rahamim rushed home; there he found the doctor who diagnosed Rabbinas's condition as a sunstroke and high blood pressure. The physician gave him an injection and prescribed a few drugs.

When Rabbinas opened his eyes, he called his wife: "You were right, Esther, I shouldn't have done it. And what's worse, they told me that the pay was ridiculously low and it was given as a disguised charity. The poor man, Dahan, his wife . . ."

"What?" asked Esther.

"Oh, nothing, nothing," he answered.

Rahamim was very unhappy. He had no friends and was learning nothing. He had seen other boys drop out of school to join their fathers in the humiliating *dahak* work which offered no future. He was determined to escape their fate. He was quite well aware that education was the key that opened all doors. Yet, what kind of education was he getting? A nothing, an absolute nothing. He decided, without consulting his father, to write his brother David and tell him about the state of affairs, the fruitlessness of his education in the village, and his father's misadventure, asking him to come as soon as possible.

Friday afternoon, Rahamim waited patiently at the bus station and wasn't disappointed. David hugged him and asked about his father's health.

"We were all worried," said Rahamim. "Now he is better, but he must still stay in bed for a week. I think we should leave this God-forsaken place. In the city it would be better for everybody. Father could find work there that's to his liking, and I hope to find a decent high school. If I don't leave this village, I'll wind up like the other kids here, in this horrible *dahak*. I even refuse to accept the idea."

David listened silently, fearing his father's objections, and decided not to promise anything. "Let's see what the old man thinks," he said.

Rahamim took his brother's answer as an indication of approval. When they were with their father, he repeated his speech with conviction, encouraged by "That's true, my son is right" interjections on the part of his mother, with whom he had beforehand discussed his plans.

When he finished, his father raised his head and stared right into his oldest son's eyes. "David, my son," he said, "I think my own personal career is over. I've already lived; I've had the privilege of coming here. This is the Holy Land, that's for sure, the land which was trodden upon by our fathers Abraham, Isaac and Jacob and our kings David and Solomon. The land of *Beth Hamikdash*, our holy Temple. I wish I could say the same about the people who live here, God forgive them." Then, after a pause, he added: "Think only of the welfare of your brother and sister, and of their future. Is Rahamim right?"

"Yes, Dad, completely. This place is neither for you nor for him. A talented boy like him will be wasted here. I've come to ask you to live with me in the city. We will live together as we did before, there, and we will share expenses, if you wish. Believe me, Dad, it won't be bad for me, and also, it's only temporary. Everything will work out, I assure you. I am thinking of Rahamim in particular. I know the high school principal very well; he is one of our bank's customers. It's a fine school, and Rahamim will find his level there. Say yes, please, Father."

Rabbinas nodded his head. "Temporarily, David; don't forget. You should not sacrifice yourself for us. You are getting along in years. You've got to get married and have children."

That Friday evening and during the Sabbath, Rahamim lived in joyful hope. He had forgotten his disappointments and looked forward to the future.

Chapter Eleven

Hadera is a small town on the Mediterranean coast halfway between Haifa and Tel Aviv. David Levy had lived there since 1949 in a small, neat, and fashionable apartment. With a bit of rearranging, he thought, the family could stay there without too much crowding. And thanks to his mother's astute management of household affairs, they could even live there comfortably.

It was in August 1958 that the family came to Hadera. September was not far off, and Rahamim was getting ready for the new academic year. He had studied during the vacation to get up to date. He was placed in the second year of high school, equivalent, at least in theory, to the eighth year of the village school. But what a difference in the students' appearance, their behavior, their respect for the teacher, the curriculum, and the level of studies! Rahamim had to "hit the books" in order to keep up with his classwork. He went at it with a will for the first two semesters.

At the end of the year, he won several prizes. He was among the top students and had hit his former stride. "What a waste it would have been to have left your brother in the village," said the principal one day to David, who was proudly following his brother's progress. "Rahamim has a brilliant future ahead of him. He must keep on with his efforts. I know that it won't be easy for you, but any sacrifice will be worthwhile."

"I'll do all in my power to help him," replied David. "But

you know that my father isn't working, and that the whole family is my responsibility."

"I will try to get your case before the school committee," promised the principal, "and I hope to be able to cut his tuition fees in half. We do that as an exception for brilliant students who can't afford the high fees. Rahamim certainly qualifies on both counts."

The principal kept his word, and David received a bill which, although cut in half, still represented a major expense in the family budget. But Rahamim fulfilled all expectations. He was top-notch in everything but was exceptionally gifted in math and science. The engineering profession caught his fancy: building, inventing, being one of the pioneers in this little country which had to be developed and consolidated. He worked hard and passed his examinations with flying colors. At the end of his third school year, he got a full scholarship for the final two years.

David was relieved. He could at last draw a free breath and think a little about himself. But he never ceased to encourage his brother, backing up his ambitions and desires. 'Rahamim will be an engineer,' he often repeated to himself. He had to, for his own sake, for the family's, for the country's. He had to show everyone that the "cave dwellers" could succeed at the highest level if only given the means. 'Ah,' he sighed joyfully, 'what would have become of my brother if I had left him in that village?'

Rahamim's scholastic achievement was not matched by social success. Many of his classmates saw in him a bookworm, a grind who did nothing but study. Rahamim very rarely went out with them. This situation now was the opposite of what it had been in the village. Here, he was embarrassed by his clothing, which was clean but pretty old-fashioned. He was not in a position to spend money like water, as his classmates did, and he preferred to stay home when they went out to have fun. They enjoyed a fat family allowance, and their pockets were always full. He always refused the spending money his brother offered him. When David insisted, Rahamim politely thanked him and declined his offer, stressing that it was enough to provide for the basic family needs.

Rahamim never knew the carefree games and amusements of adolescence. He was an adult before his time, and his precocious maturity alienated him even more from boys his own age. He despised the pampered family pets, the mediocre students who hated school but were forced to attend by their status-conscious, wealthy parents. With girls he was even more withdrawn. They admired his intelligence and his academic talents, but after class hours, he was not for them. He had never dated a girl and satisfied her thirst for spending.

Rahamim was the only Oriental in his class. His name betrayed his origin. He wore it like a flag and he always resisted the temptation to shorten it or to europeanize it. One day, one of his classmates bluntly said: "Rami is a rather common name. That sounds a whole lot better than Rahamim. Rami Levy, what a nice combination! Ra-ha-mim sounds too Oriental, too Arab, especially that guttural *ha*, so hard to pronounce after the initial *Ra*."

"I like it the way it is," replied Rahamim, a bit angered. "Choosing a name is the father's privilege; a name is like a relic and must be kept intact. Besides, why should we hide our identity? There's nothing to be ashamed of." He did make one concession, however; he let his schoolmates call him Rami. Later on, he himself stopped pronouncing his name gutturally as his father did. He wasn't exactly sure if it was by deliberate choice or by unconscious habit. He only remembered the scornful laughter that would greet him in class when he was still a newcomer and the embarrassment in which he often found himself because of his name and his Oriental accent. By a natural habit, he began to speak like his schoolmates, and, although he never tried to consciously hide his background, he was flattered when a stranger mistook him for a native Israeli, a *sabra*. His physical appearance lent itself to that. He was fair-complected, with brown hair and green eyes; he was tall, well-built, and strongly resembled the generation of Jews who were born in freedom.

In the spring of 1962, Rahamim passed his examinations

successfully. The road was clear for his engineering career. In June, 1966, after four years of study at the technological institute, he received his engineering degree *summa cum laude*. He was twenty-three years old. Two months later, he was mustered into the army, and after his basic training and an arduous course for officers, he was transferred to a scientific research center run by the army in the north of the country.

Chapter Twelve

It was very cold in the barracks, and an icy wind blew fiercely. The winter of 1967 was drawing to a close. Lieutenant Rahamim Levy had received orders to report to this station to help with the installation of ultra-modern electronic equipment which the army had just acquired. It was his field, electronics, and he got along well in it. The equipment was very effective but also very intricate, and Levy, the engineer, had the job of setting up the training program for new recruits in the management of these precious machines.

In the center of this military camp, facing the mess hall, a little masonry building housed the unit's offices. Uri, the liaison officer, hung up his telephone and turned to his secretary. "Shlomit," he said, "they've just told me that a Lieutenant Levy will arrive this afternoon. Please tell all the officers and soldiers in the unit to be here at two o'clock. We don't have any time to waste. The colonel's order is 'Rush! Rush!' He wants to see the equipment in operation in three or four weeks at the latest. Good functioning will save many lives."

Corporal Shlomit Weiss immediately carried out the order.

At two o'clock, fifteen men gathered at the office. All waited impatiently. Up until then, they had only read one or two articles on the first-rate quality of the equipment which they had to operate. They were eager to see it, to touch it, and they were very proud to have been selected to serve in this new unit. A few minutes later, a jeep let Lieutenant Rahamim Levy off in front of the office. Uri introduced him to the group. Everybody's eyes were fixed on the young engineer who commanded the secrets of these devices, the very last word in modern military science, which they would soon master and operate.

Rahamim answered their questioning gaze with an eloquent smile, but his eyes rested on Shlomit. In a furtive glance, he looked her over from head to foot. Shlomit was very embarrassed. Without looking at him, she held her hand out for the envelope which the lieutenant was giving her and which contained his personal file. With a quick movement, he prevented her from getting it. He clutched the envelope in his hand, stammering: "Wait a moment, please. I have some papers to get out of the envelope."

Shlomit held back and said in a nervous voice, "Excuse me. I thought you were going to give it to me." As she talked, their eyes met and she blushed.

"Here it is," Rahamim said, giving her the envelope. "My whole life is in there. Take good care of it."

All of this lasted only a few seconds. Then the commander ordered: "Let's get to work, friends; we're in a hurry." Everybody left. Shlomit stayed in the office with Uri, the liaison officer of the unit which henceforth would count Rahamim Levy as one of its officers.

Uri was in his fortieth year. He was a career officer, a former paratrooper, and had been transferred to desk work after sustaining a serious wound. He didn't much like it. Actually, Shlomit ran the show, and he completely trusted his secretary whom he held in high regard. He admired her for her beauty, and he liked her for her intelligence and devotion. A close and sincere relationship developed between them.

He asked her bluntly: "Shlomit, I noticed that you blushed and that you were very embarrassed. Have you met Lieutenant Levy before?"

"No, Uri," answered the young girl, "I've never seen him before in my life, and I don't know what got hold of me. As soon as he came, I felt a tremor mounting all through me as if I had just received an electric shock. And when my eyes met his, something lit up in me and the flame went right to my face.

It's the first time that I've experienced this kind of feeling."

In a friendly way, Uri teased: "It must be love, my little girl, love at first sight, as you sometimes encounter in novels or in movies. As I often told you, I've never felt anything like that. I was so busy making war that I never had time to love. But, for you, a beautiful nineteen-year-old girl, it is different. Love, my dear, enjoy your life!"

'Is that really love?' Shlomit wondered, stretched out on her bed, her big eyes wide open in the dark of the night. It was two o'clock in the morning, and Levy's face hadn't left her for a moment. She tried to find an explanation. 'I've never seen him before,' she said to herself; 'I don't know him at all. How can you love someone without having met him before?' By strenuous mental effort, she tried to analyze her feelings. She thought through all the theories of magnetism, hypnotic suggestion, telepathy, but nothing was good enough to set her mind at ease and put her to sleep. A force inside her worked powerfully on her nervous system and completely overwhelmed her. "I have to see him again," she heard herself say decisively; "this is the only way to understand." She thought of a second meeting with the young engineer, and the scene as she envisioned it had a sedative effect on her. After a few minutes, her eyes closed and she fell into deep sleep.

The next day, she woke up with a start two hours later than usual and immediately telephoned Uri. At first, she wanted to tell him that she wouldn't be in the office, then she reconsidered. Urgent work was waiting for her, and she also wanted to solve the mystery of the night before. So she told her boss that she would be late. Before hanging up, Uri didn't miss the opportunity to say that Engineer Levy was in the office and that he absolutely wanted to see her. 'That's good,' she thought, 'he too got hit. We've both been struck by the same bolt of lightning.' A feeling of joy overwhelmed her. She dressed quickly, gulped down a glass of milk on her way out, and told her mother that she couldn't wait and would eat in the barracks. Then she headed toward the bus station, and jumped into the huge vehicle which had just started off.

"Somebody's in a hurry," the driver said jokingly. "You could have been crushed, Miss Corporal. What's the rush? Has war broken out?"

"No, Mister driver, not war, love!"

Rahamim Levy went back to the office before lunch and found Shlomit looking through his personal file. When she saw him, she was embarrassed at her indiscretion and began to stammer excuses and explanations. But Levy quickly put her at ease, saying that insofar as she was a very dedicated secretary, she had to know all the secrets, that he had nothing to hide, and that she could find everything out if she only agreed to see him more often. Shlomit smiled, relieved.

"I only had time to see your birthdate; for a young man of twenty-four, you've achieved quite a lot," she ventured.

"Oh yes, I have worked hard," the young officer remarked. "I've had a little bit of luck, too. Let's talk about it later. I came to ask you to have lunch with me. We will have an opportunity to get to know each other."

Shlomit didn't need any more coaxing. "Of course," she said, "that fits in just right. I haven't had anything to eat this morning." As she said that, she remembered her conversation with Uri who had informed her of the young man's first visit.

"You know that I came to see you this morning in the office," Rahamim said as if he had been reading her thoughts.

"What? Oh, yes, Uri mentioned it to me. Did you need anything?"

"No," he answered, "I only wanted to see you."

"I'm ready," Shlomit said, putting on her coat. "We can leave now."

"Let's go to the officers' mess," Rahamim suggested.

The meal was very simple. They had salami sandwiches and orange juice. They ate in silence, at times interrupted with general observations about barracks life, its joys and its pains. Then, they spoke of the military situation on the Syrian front, of the kibbutzim in the valley which were at the mercy of the Syrian artillery on the Golan Heights, and of the heroism of the Israeli pilots who had just shot down several enemy planes. The two companions agreed on the gravity of the situation. Both were sure that the army was ready for any contingency and that the state of quasi peace which the country was enjoying was preferable to total war, which could only lead to destruction and death on both sides.

"Let's change the subject, will you?" Rahamim said. "War or no war, that doesn't depend on us. We'll do what we have to do in due time. Let's speak about us and what depends on us. Let's . . ."

"Do you think there is anything which really depends on us," interrupted Shlomit, "anything we can change?"

"Of course," answered Rahamim, still fresh from his scientific training. "Man enjoys free will; he constantly has to make choices. A great deal depends on himself; this is precisely what distinguishes Judaism from Islam, whose attitude towards life is fatalistic. It may be a comfortable attitude, since man can rely on a supreme power, on God, and accept with serenity all the misfortunes that befall him. But it is hostile to progress and it is certainly at the root of the present underdevelopment of the Arab countries and the decline of their civilization, which, in the past, knew periods of grandeur. The Jewish formula is different: God foresees everything, but man has freedom of choice. If we didn't have freedom, we would be like the child in the Arab tale who, after killing his father and mother, asks the judge for mercy because God has made him an orphan."

Shlomit listened to this long monologue with admiration mixed with astonishment. She knew of his scientific aptitudes, and there he was, now, a philosopher and a sociologist. She had never attained such a degree of learning. She knew nothing about Islam and almost nothing about the Arab world surrounding her, and it was difficult for her to imagine the past "grandeur" of the Arab "civilization." For her, as for those in her

71

generation, the Arab was an enemy to be vanquished and against whom it was necessary to be militarily prepared in order to avoid another holocaust. The Arab's refusal to accept the existence of Israel, and particularly their leaders' repeated vows to destroy the Jewish State and drive the Jews into the sea, had the reverse effect of reinforcing this resolve and of strengthening the military might of the small nation in permanent state of siege. The military successes of the young state and the heroism of its youth gave rise to feelings of superiority over the Arabs, whose image was that of a backward people, a prey to ignorance and disease, fanatical to the extreme and always beaten in the wars they provoked.

"Where did you learn all this?" she asked her companion after a period of meditation. "Not in high school, of course; maybe in the Institute?"

"Oh, no," the officer answered, "it's from my father."

"From your father!" she exclaimed. "You're lucky! Mine taught me nothing, and if he speaks of grandeur, he knows only one, that of the Jews . . . of . . . Europe, of Eastern Europe. I think it will do him a lot of good to hear something else. As for myself, I wish I could read more about the subject."

"I appreciate your interest in reading and studying," Rahamim answered. "But, even more, I admire your beautiful eyes and your charming smile, the sweetness of your voice, and the elegance of your figure. That's what I intended to talk to you about, because from the moment my eyes met yours, something quivered in me, and I haven't stopped thinking about you and desiring to be with you."

Shlomit lowered her eyes. Would she confess her own feelings? That might be premature and sound phony as if, out of politeness, she were paying him the same honor. He had taken her by surprise, and she hadn't expected this admission on the first date. Ah, how she wanted to be the first to take him into her confidence! Now that he had beaten her to it, she chose silence and put an end to this uncomfortable situation. She glanced furtively at her watch, reminding the young man that he had to return to work.

"Oh," he exclaimed, "I don't want to be late. I hope I haven't bored you. Today is . . . Thursday, and I'll be free on Saturday. If you have no objection, we could get together on Saturday. Do you like to swim? Would you go with me to the beach?"

This avalanche of questions surprised the young girl and added to her confusion. She couldn't answer; was it her timidity or an instinctive fear to go too far too soon? She finally muttered: "No . . . no, not so soon, maybe another time."

The lieutenant persisted; "I will call you tomorrow," he said. "I hope that by then, you will have changed your mind."

The telephone rang. Uri was away, and Shlomit was alone at the office. She grabbed the receiver and was relieved to hear Rami's voice asking her if she was well and if she had changed her mind. "Yes," she replied mechanically. The engineer immediately set the time and place for the date. When she hung up, she realized that she hadn't said a word, changed a detail, or expressed any reservations. For the first time in her life, she was going to spend an entire day alone with a man for whom she felt something she had never experienced before, a man she had only known for three days and who seemed attracted to her by the same invisible and overwhelming force. 'Why must I torture myself this way?' she wondered. 'I commend to my prayers and devotion this happy moment. I am no longer a child; this had to happen one day. If it has been very quick, so what? My feelings are very strong, and suppressing them will make me suffer even more.' Obviously satisfied with her rationalization, she cried out in the empty office: "Take heart, Shlomit! Until Saturday, my love!"

Lieutenant Levy spent all day Friday in a military installation far away. He had worked thirteen hours in a row, checking with other technicians the safety devices of the electronic weapons deployed along the border. At nightfall, he had a very late meal and dropped on his bed, exhausted. His work was not over, and he knew it. His commander had offered him the lab keys in case he wanted to go in there on Saturday, the weekly day of rest. The hint was obvious; it was a thinly disguised order to the lieutenant to give up his Sabbath for "the national war effort." Lieutenant Levy had done that before, but this time, he stood his ground.

"I can't," he said to his commander. "I'm not free."

This laconic answer didn't seem to please his superior who replied in a menacing tone, "Ah, ah, I see, it's that corporal who has turned your head. Don't forget that she, too, as we say here, is military property, and as long as we wear the uniform, we belong to the army."

Rahamim didn't conceal his resentment: "Sir, please don't mix that girl up in our business. Moreover, allow me to remind you that this military property, as you say, is well protected by certain articles of the military code, particularly those pertaining to the number of hours in a row that can be imposed on a soldier. After all, we are not at war."

The commanding officer nodded his head grudgingly and replied firmly: "We are always at war, Levy." Then, he cut short the conversation and left Rahamim alone.

Levy woke up very early Saturday. A few hours separated him from his date with Shlomit. While he was at the Institute, and during his few months of army duty, he had often visited "the girls," but it was only to satisfy his physical needs. He enjoyed formulating theories on the bestiality of man who sought women out only to satisfy his instincts. He thought of sexual desire as a physical need like hunger, thirst, and sleep. The only difference, he believed, was in the need of a human partner of the other sex. Whether this partner was moved by the same physical drives or simply engaged in a lucrative occupation didn't in any way change man's sexual equation. Sexual contacts always remained short and transitory. Levy showed complete lack of understanding mixed with haughty pity and condescension for his friends, male and female, who were "hooked." "Love," he was often heard to say, "is good for the weak. It's the manifestation of exclusive selfishness rather than an expression of self-sacrifice because the lover attempts to dominate the personality of the other." Rahamim had always dissociated physical desire from sentimental love; for him it was a waste of time to nurture a relationship if it did not quickly lead to the sexual act, which he liked to call "the relief."

But, on that day, it was not the same Rahamim Levy, and he was well aware of the change in him. He ardently desired Shlomit's company. He was about to have her to himself for the whole day, and yet, no erotic idea ruffled his thought. Quite the contrary, he kept telling himself: I must not soil her; she's too precious; she belongs to me!

"She belongs to me?" he exclaimed out loud. "By what right? I, who used to make fun of those 'lovers,' have I become like them? Something must have changed inside of me. Why does she inspire such intense desires in me which transcend the physical, the desire to be near her, to bask in her gaze, to hear her voice, to breathe her perfume?"

What seemed strangest to him was that feeling of duty, of obligation to protect this fragile being and jealously guard her as if she were a precious jewel or a religious relic. "What right do I have?" he repeated to himself. "Why her and not another?" But he found no answer to his questions. "If that's love," he concluded, "that must be wonderful."

Chapter Thirteen

Dor is a lovely Mediterranean beach with fine golden sand stretching as far as the eye can see. The sea is always calm because the bay is sheltered by overhanging heights which block the wind. It is a favorite place for swimmers, who can at the same time enjoy the quiet water of the pool, the delights of sand and sun, and the vast expanse of sea beyond the bay.

It was still spring, and only true swimmers went to the beach this early in the season. And lovers. A few young couples were already stretched out on the sand, isolated from the rest of the world. Others played amorously in the water, between the sea and the sky, both clear blue.

Rahamim spotted a patch of shade not yet occupied and started off for it. In his right hand, he held a picnic basket which he had carefully prepared that morning. Under his left arm was a rolled-up mat. When he got to the spot, he unrolled the mat and spread it out in the shade.

"Here we are," he said to his companion; "all set for the rest of the day."

"You thought of everything," Shlomit said with a smile. "You must be used to it. How many times have you brought girls here with baskets and food?"

"Shlomit, you won't believe me. I don't know what kind of impression I'm making on you, but this is the first time I've come here with a girl, and it's the first time in my life I've fixed a picnic basket."

As he said this, a faint pink rose in his cheeks. Shlomit

interpreted this as proof of his sincerity. Nevertheless, she added, "It was silly of me to ask you such a question. After all, you were free to do what you wanted."

Rahamim was surprised by her use of the past tense. 'Does she mean I'm no longer free?' he thought. Then, aloud, he said, "You're right, I used to be free. From now on . . ."

She didn't let him continue. She understood her mistake. "No, Rahamim," she cut him short: "You are always free. We scarcely know each other." This answer put some distance between them, and a chilly silence prevailed for a moment. It was Rahamim who broke it: "Let's relax, Shlomit; let's enjoy this beautiful place."

He went from words to actions and began to undress. He took off his shirt, and unbuttoned his pants, letting them fall on the mat. Then he neatly folded his clothes and turned toward his girl friend, bare-chested in a bathing suit.

"Your turn now," he said.

Shlomit hesitated a moment out of modesty. Then she rose, unzippered her dress, and stepped out of it resplendent like a newly-hatched chick breaking out of its shell. Rahamim couldn't take his eyes off her. She wore a sky-blue bikini, edged in black, which molded her perfectly, the top tightly cupping her breasts. Her bare navel accented the shape of her smooth and firm belly, and her dimpled thighs enhanced her slender figure. The beautiful girl drew two pins from her hair and let her black mane, shining in the sunlight, fall onto her neck. Her brown skin was a sharp contrast to the fair skin of her companion.

"Shlomit," he exclaimed, "you're absolutely adorable." He came close to her, wanting to kiss her, but held back. His hand, falling on the girl's arm, inadvertently caressed her, and he felt her quiver. She was standing silent. Rahamim approached her, eagerly looked into her eyes, and said in a trembling voice, "I love you, Shlomit. I love you very much." He took her hand into his. The girl held her companion's hand tightly. It was the only response she could give. Their fingers stayed intertwined, clutching as if under the power of hypnosis, and the perspiration in their palms made the contact warm and wet. They stood for a long while, eyes closed, hand in hand. Then came the release, accompanied by a sensation of well-being.

Shlomit raised her eyes; they were moist. Then she lowered her head and let it rest under his chin. Protectively, Rahamim encircled the girl's head with his right arm and pressed her against him. She, in turn, hugged him. Her arms went around his waist, and he felt, crushing against his chest, the upraised hardened nipples of her quivering breasts. He felt as though he were drifting away in a whirlwind of sensuousness. A sweep of blood and a quivering of nerves washed over his body. He gently pushed away the lock of hair which covered her nape. She responded to this stimulation, raising her head toward her companion; he in turn lowered his. Their mouths were open, their breath panting.

Quickly he kissed her moist eyes. Then he let his lips wander on her cheek as far as the corner of her mouth. Shlomit lifted her mouth, and their lips joined voluptuously in their first kiss.

Rahamim was the first to break the embrace. He didn't want to go any further. Now that she was his, he wanted to keep her pure, virginal, until the wedding night if she agreed to be his wife. It was the sacred custom among his people, and he found it right. He didn't know what Shlomit would think about it, nor was he sure of the reaction of her parents. He saw how inexperienced she was in love, how she quivered, her eyes moist with tears.

"Let's take a little break, Shlomit, my love," he suggested. "Let's calm down and relish the serenity of love."

"Yes, darling," answered the girl. "these have been the happiest moments of my life. I have never before felt the power of love. It's the first time."

"Shlomit dear, it is my first time, too, the first time I have known real love."

"You know, Rami," she said, "when you came into my office the other day, I wanted to tell you that I loved you from the first moment I saw you. But you beat me to it, and I didn't have the courage to repeat your own words after you. I was afraid you wouldn't believe me. Ever since then, I've been hiding my feelings, burdened by the suppressed desire to confess. Now it's off my chest, and I feel relieved."

Rahamim didn't hide his pleasure and solemnly declared, "Shlomit, my darling, we are bound by our first kiss. We have sworn to belong to each other."

The day went by quickly for the lovers. Both were good swimmers and enjoyed diving, jumping, splashing each other, and stretching out side by side for a sunbath. Now and then, they went rummaging in the picnic basket and they ate ravenously.

"The air here whets the appetite," said Shlomit.

"Yes, but don't forget, my dear, the presence of a beloved companion. If each of us had come alone . . ."

"You'd have to be crazy to come here alone in May. I thought you were joking when you asked me to spend the day at the beach. In fact, I wasn't sure if I wanted it or not. But now I am very glad I accepted your invitation. You've given me the most beautiful day of my life."

"Of our life," stressed the lieutenant, "our life together. Nothing will ever separate us."

"Yes, Rami, nothing will separate us. Nothing."

Everyone at the army base admired this couple; the two seemed so well matched. They were seen as a symbol of the Israeli melting pot. Judging by their physical appearances, one would think that Shlomit was the Sephardi and Rami, the Ashkenazi. But their names proved otherwise. "Levy" might be neutral, but "Rahamim" was definitely Oriental. And while "Shlomit" was nonindicative, "Weiss" was doubtless of European origin.

The couple got along marvelously and made no case for ethnic differences. Shlomit saw in this union a realization of her Baudelairean dream. Rahamim was the "unknown," the "new" that she sought and she was happy to find "Heaven" rather than "Hell." For he was a handsome lad, bright and well-educated, very well thought of in the army, and, most importantly, he was genuine and loving. As for Rahamim, he was enthralled by the beauty and the freshness of this pure and sensible girl who cherished him sincerely. He was more aware than she was of the difficulties their families would meet in getting along, no less understanding one another. In his prep school years, when he was the only North African in a class of Europeans, he could detect a certain arrogant scorn, particularly from the older generation. He could never forget one of those monthly open forums in his class during which they discussed the poverty of North African inhabitants in the neighboring villages and the need to collect old winter clothes for their children. He had become the focal point of the class which saw him as the representative of these poor neighbors. In his heart he hated those "philanthropists," their condescension and their paternalism. He had chosen to remain silent, but when one of the committee members suggested that Rahamim Levy head the delegation that would take the old clothes to the village, he couldn't hold it back: "I refuse to accept this role," he said, "because I believe that every citizen has a right to a job and a decent standard of living. If these poor people don't have clothes, it's a shame on us all and on the government. It is not charity they need, it is justice. Instead of leaving them without jobs and unable to provide for themselves so that the privileged *nouveaux riches* could appease their consciences by giving them charity, the government should have secured work for them and ensured a basic minimal income that would make your humiliating alms unnecessary. Don't forget that among the new rich of today, many arrived only a few years ago without a penny, and it is the same government and its unjust system of favoritism that made them rich. They are now playing at philanthropy. No, I am against this vile action and I move that this class send a petition to the government. I demand that my motion be put to the vote." Levy's motion was defeated by a wide margin. Only one of his classmates voted with him and was soon accused of being a communist.

In his family and at the homes of their North African friends,

Rahamim often heard endless complaints about discrimination against them, and favoritism, or *protecsia*, as they called it, for the *voosvoos*. He was aware that education was a basic element and a prerequisite for a successful melting pot that would bring together the lost "tribes" which had been separated by a multisecular abyss, and he was sure his brilliant scholastic career would serve as a bridge over this gap. A little cynical pride was mixed in the thread of his relationship with Shlomit. After all, he thought, Shlomit was only a high school graduate. Her parents, she once told him, hadn't even finished elementary school in their native countries. But in his family, his mother had graduated from a French school, and his father was very learned in Hebrew and Arabic.

Encouraged by his analysis, he informed Shlomit of his desire to ask her parents for her hand. She acquiesced joyfully, and she was sure her parents would be delighted. The young lovers had been going steady for five weeks and had been seeing each other every day. She often returned home very late at night, and her parents, evidently worried, questioned her at length about her company and told her they would welcome her friends in their house. Shlomit was usually very evasive, but one day, at the insistence of her mother, she declared, "I have a boyfriend, an officer, an engineer, and we are in love."

"Can we know his name?" inquired her father.

"Levy," answered the girl.

"Why don't you invite him for dinner some evening?" said her mother. "Is it serious, Shlomit? You know you are of age. We are getting old and would like to see you married and settled."

"Please, Mother, let's not talk about that. I am only nineteen; we don't have to rush things. Besides, it is for him to take the first step."

Now the first step had been taken, and Shlomit accepted enthusiastically. "As a matter of fact," she told her lover, "my parents have always wanted to invite you home, but I was not sure you would accept the invitation."

"With great pleasure," Rahamim replied with a smile.

81

Chapter Fourteen

Lieutenant Levy knocked at the door. The apartment was located on the third floor of a new building where the family had moved a few months earlier. Shlomit opened the door; she was radiant in a pink dress. She immediately introduced him to her parents who seemed gratified and exchanged meaningful glances as if to say: "Shlomit has made a good choice; here is our future son-in-law." Levy gave Mrs. Weiss the bouquet of flowers he had in his hand and everybody sat down at the table. They talked about the political situation, and the conversation quickly devolved on the incumbent leadership which Mendel Weiss constantly praised. Levy seemed less satisfied and accused the government of certain derelictions and the political regime of corruption. Gita tried to turn the conversation to less inflammatory topics. She didn't want to jeopardize her daughter's chances of marrying such a nice man.

"Well," said Mendel, "I see that you are pretty well informed about politics. We can't sell you this pre-election garbage as we do once in four years, before elections, to these ignorant and backward North African immigrants."

Levy suddenly stopped chewing his food. This unconscious gesture was not noticed by Mendel who went on: "What a tremendous job we have, to educate these primitive people and get them used to the democratic system; to bring them from the dark Middle Ages to the enlightened twentieth century."

Shlomit blushed beet red. She realized her mistake: she should have told her parents about the background of their future son-in-law. She had deliberately concealed this detail, precisely, she thought, so that their opinion of him would be objective, so that they could judge him on his own merits. True, she was aware of her father's prejudices, but she couldn't imagine he would be so stupid as to tell it all to his guest and future son-in-law the first hour of their meeting. She tried to blunt her father's statement: "Rami," she said, "my father is obsessed with the idea of educating everybody as if God had entrusted him with this great civilizing mission. But I believe, as goes the saying, that charity begins at home."

Mendel Weiss smiled. "It's true, my little one, you are right. I merely wanted to show Mr. Levy my small contribution to the assimilation of the new immigrants into the mainstream of our society. I'm sure that a man as educated and as well learned as Mr. Levy . . . by the way, what is your first name, Mr. Levy? And may I call you by your first name?"

"Rami . . ." Shlomit answered instantly.

Levy cut off her response with his own: "My name is Rahamim," he said, stressing intentionally the guttural part which he had ceased to pronounce for many years.

The name had a horrible effect on Mendel. He couldn't swallow the mouthful of water he had just taken and was gripped with a fit of choking accompanied with hopeless gestures. His forehead and temples broke out in a sweat. His wife had to escort him to his room where he slowly recovered his calm.

"I don't know what happened to me," he said, ashamed, when he returned to the table. "Please excuse me and finish your meal in peace."

Alone, face to face, Shlomit and her lover exchanged glances full of sadness and wonder. "Does that happen often?" the young man asked ironically.

"Yes, these fits have become very frequent recently," she answered, unable to cover up her embarrassment. "He lost a lung during the war," she added, apparently satisfied to find an excuse.

"Which war?" the young man asked.

"The war of independence, 1948."

83

"What an unfortunate coincidence," Levy sighed, "just when I pronounced my first name. Maybe this was the cause . . ."

Shlomit knew quite well that Rahamim was right. She was aware of her father's prejudices, but she thought that Rahamim's diploma and high rank in the army would largely make up for what her racist father might consider his lack of pedigree. She was wrong but deliberately lied in hopes of protecting their love. "No, Rami, I don't think so," she murmured, "your name has nothing to do . . ."

For the same reason, Rahamim accepted his lover's explanation. "Well," he said, "I'm sorry about this embarrassing incident. It's getting late, and I must leave. Have a good night. See you tomorrow." He came close to Shlomit and kissed her gently on her quivering lips.

The next day, Shlomit didn't go to the mess hall for lunch as she did every day. This troubled Rahamim. He waited until the last moment and, without eating his meal, ran to her office. She was sitting at her desk, her two fists tightly clenched under her chin, her eyes empty and dreamy. Levy stared at her for a moment, then yelled her name, which made the girl jump.

"I waited for you at lunch. What's going on? Are you angry with me?"

"No," she replied without raising her head, "just the opposite. I'm ashamed, really ashamed."

"Ashamed of what?" he asked.

"Ashamed of my father and his prejudices. Ashamed, too, of having lied to you to cover them up. Ashamed of having deliberately hidden from my parents the truth about your background. Ashamed! Ashamed! And I can't look you in the eye now."

Rahamim knew her hypersensitivity and her sincerity, and he loved her all the more for them. "I lied to you, too," he said, "in pretending to accept your explanation. So we're even. Let's stop kidding around and be more serious. Shlomit, darling, I don't care what your parents think or say. If you still love me, that's all that really matters. And if you agree to marry me, I'm

84

asking for your hand here and now. If you can be a corporal in the Israeli army, you can certainly pick your husband."

Shlomit threw her arms around his neck and kissed him passionately as if to thank him for this wonderful surprise. She had thought he was piqued by her father's behavior, and here he was, on the contrary, consoling her. She lifted her eyes, and asked bluntly, "And your parents? Will I see them? What will they say?"

"Don't worry about my parents. They are of a different breed. They're not wealthy but they are certainly very nice and warm people. You'll see them, of course. Next week, if you wish."

"Rami, my father had my mother tell me that he is opposed to our marriage and that he would not attend the wedding ceremony if I got married against his will."

"And your mother?"

"She doesn't agree with him. She constantly suffers from his behavior. She told him that she would be present at the wedding of her only daughter, without him, if necessary."

"And what do you think?" he asked.

"I should have a heart-to-heart talk with my father. Maybe I can convince him. At least, I must try . . ."

"I wish you good luck," said Rahamim. "And if it doesn't work? . . ."

"My mind is made up," affirmed Shlomit. "I will be your wife, with his blessing, or without."

Her appeal to Mendel was fruitless. He stood like a rock. "Education," he told his daughter, "is skin-deep; it does not change the personality. Nature is stronger; innate qualities never disappear."

Gita lost her patience. She was sickened by the hypocrisy of her husband who certainly knew the "nature" and the "innate qualities" of his daughter. She opened her mouth but Shlomit was faster: "What are those 'innate qualities' of the Levys which make you seem so afraid?" said the girl, restraining her disdain and revulsion.

"I've already said it in a long conversation with you, you

should remember. Those Oriental people are like Arabs, and I will not accept them in my family."

"Mendel, you are completely crazy," said his wife vigorously. "You seem to forget . . ."

"Forget what?" he asked cynically.

Gita was unable to hold back the violent sobs that shook her. She could no longer hide the secret that had been choking her for nineteen years. Mendel's effrontery had finally pushed her to the breaking point. "You seem to forget that Shlomit isn't our real daughter," she yelled, "and that we adopted her, and that her nature . . ." Gita stopped short; the whole truth would have killed her daughter.

"Stop, Gita, you've gone mad," Mendel screamed at his wife. He had been accustomed to relying on her discretion, and this had allowed him to vent his cynicism and hypocrisy.

"No, I must speak out!" exclaimed the poor woman. "Forgive me, Shlomit, my child, my little beloved daughter, for not having told you this secret which has been eating away at me. He is the one who has always prevented me from . . ."

Before Gita could finish her sentence, she dropped on the couch and passed out.

Shlomit was stunned. This revelation was too brutal. She had always loved her mother, and she got up now to get something for her to drink. 'This is my mother, the only mother I know,' she thought. When Gita opened her eyes, the two women hugged each other tightly and sobbed. Mendel stood, embarrassed by the tender affection from which he was excluded. He humbly lowered his head and, without even a backward glance, walked out of the room and closed the door behind him.

After she fully recovered, Gita looked at her daughter through tear-filled eyes which reflected a life of suffering. She felt pity for this fragile being on whom she'd lavished care and love. She was truly her daughter, the only living person in the world whom she loved and for whom she strove to live in spite of her delicate health. No, she would not reveal the rest; she must not. It was enough for the poor girl to learn abruptly that she had lived a lie all this time. At any price, she had to keep

Shlomit from learning the truth about her ethnic parentage, a truth that could certainly be fatal to her. 'I will take this secret with me to the grave,' she decided. She raised her head toward the girl and her frightened gaze met Shlomit's wide-open and inquisitive eyes.

"Why did you adopt me? Who are my real parents?" Shlomit asked fiercely.

"My daughter—as long as I live, I will call you my daughter—how much pain and agony I would have spared if I hadn't followed the capricious orders of your father!"

"You mean Mendel Weiss," Shlomit interrupted. "Now that I have the choice, I don't want him for my father."

"I can't blame you," answered Gita, "you are of age now, and free to make your own choices. But I must tell you that, though I may have been the cause of your adoption, it was your father . . . I mean, . . . Mendel . . . who got the idea. I have already told you about my awful experience in the Nazi concentration camp. What I have concealed from you, because it is horrible to say and to listen to, is that, like many other Jewish women, I was used as a guinea pig by Nazi scientists to test their accursed theories. I came out of that inferno sterile."

"Oh, my God!" exclaimed Shlomit, terribly upset. "What a horrible thing! What cruelty, what foul humanity, what a disgusting existence, nothing but misfortune and pain!" Then, after a pause, she firmly reiterated, "Who are my parents and where are they?"

"I don't know who they are," stammered Gita. "We heard that they were dead, or that they couldn't be found. It was Mendel who brought you one day and left you in my care. It was during the war. He told me that you had been abandoned. At first, I cared for you out of pity. Then we adopted you legally, you see . . ."

"During the war, you said? Where did he find me?"

Gita was sorry to have mentioned this detail. Against her will, she went on lying in order to cover up her mistake and to keep her daughter from the slightest hint that would lead her

87

closer to the truth. "In Tel Aviv," she said hesitatingly, assured that it was the only exclusively Jewish city in the world.

Shlomit didn't seem convinced by this confession, but she felt pity for the wretched woman. She suspected her of not telling the whole story, but what could she do? The idea of hunting out her origins came to her, but where to start and how? She had no clue, no key to open the door of this mystery. One thing was certain: she could no longer look in the eye of this haughty and surly man, this stuck-up racist who had imposed on her his paternity from which she had just freed herself. "Now I understand why I don't look like you," she said. "Maybe I was born into one of those Oriental tribes to whom your husband has consecrated his pathological hate and scorn."

"Maybe," said her mother, reassured.

"Well," said the girl with pride, "there I am going to return." She felt something inside her violently pushing her towards her lover. "Rami!" she screamed, as she ran out of the house. "Rahamim! Rahamim!"

Rahamim was stretched out on his bed, his eyes wide open. For several days, the situation at the borders had been explosive, and war, total war, seemed imminent. He had been allowed to return to his room after a long period of exhausting work at the base. But he knew quite well that a telegram or a messenger would come at any moment and call him back to the barracks. The lieutenant was thinking about the Arab-Israeli conflict, its beginnings and the probability of war, if the Arab leaders decided to impose it on his little country. Like his fellow countrymen, he was sure that the Arabs would be beaten as in '48, as in '56. This unshakable faith was paradoxically fed by the unique geopolitical situation of his country, for which military defeat meant annihilation. "*Ein Breira*," he said aloud, "We have no choice."

He raised his eyes and was surprised to see Shlomit standing in the doorway, which was half-open because of the heat. He jumped down off the bed and took her in his arms. She didn't move. Her hair was undone, her blouse unbuttoned. Her eyes were haggard and had lost their brightness. Rami led her into the room and closed the door.

"What's the matter?" he asked apprehensively. "What happened? Do you feel sick?"

She remained dumb. Her face was pale, her hands cold.

"Do you want me to call a doctor, darling?" he asked. She shook her head. Rami seated her on his bed, helped her lie down fully clothed and put a woolen blanket over her. "I'll get you something to drink," he said. He looked for some tea bags but didn't find any. Then he spotted an almost-empty bottle of cognac, grabbed it, and poured out its contents into a glass. "Here, take a swallow," he urged her. "It will buck you up; it will calm you and warm you. After that, you'll tell me what's upsetting you. Fear nothing, my love; I am here, with you."

This was the first time that Shlomit had come to his room. Faithful to his beliefs and to the promise he had made to himself, Rami never urged her to come to his room. It seemed strange to him to find himself alone with her at night, the door locked, and a glass of cognac in her hand.

Shlomit gulped it down in one swallow. At first, she grimaced, then a feeling of well-being swept over her. The color came back to her face. She stared at her companion, then motioned for him to come closer to her. Rahamim was astonished at the change; he came silently to the edge of the bed. Shlomit sat up and took his hand. "Thank you, my dear," she smiled. "You are my only reason for living."

"Why? What happened, Shlomit?"

"Rami, Rami, I am no longer myself. I am someone else. My father is not my father, my mother is not my mother. Nothing, nothing. I don't belong to the Weisses."

"I can't understand anything of what you are saying. This is a riddle. My father is pretty good at it, not I."

"It isn't a riddle, Rahamim, it's true, it's true. She just told me about it."

"Who is she, and what has she just told you?" Rahamim inquired, puzzled.

"She, she, the woman who was my mother."

"What? She isn't your mother? You mean you were adopted?"

Shlomit nodded yes. The lieutenant tried to hide his surprise and, to comfort her, he said, "And that's the cause of your bewilderment! Come on now, it isn't a misfortune. The world is full of adopted children, and believe me, they are often happier than natural offspring. And besides, you are no longer a child."

"For nineteen years, I've been living with a lie. I don't even know who I am. Why did they hide the truth from me? How can I go on living without knowing who my real parents are, and what my real name is?"

"Calm down, darling. As soon as you feel better, I will take you home. And I give you my word that I will do everything I can to help you discover your real identity. As far as I am concerned, whoever you are, it changes nothing. Whether you come from the North Pole or even from the moon, you will always be my first, my only love," declared Rahamim. Then, noticing the good effect of his words on Shlomit, he added, "Now, do you want me to accompany you home?"

"No, no! I've already told her that he would never see me again. You know that I have a bed at the base, unless . . ."

As she spoke, she looked around the room. Rami understood and said: "We are about to get married, my darling; you'll be my wife. My room is yours. I'll leave you the keys."

"No, no, Rahamim," she begged, "I am afraid to stay alone. I need you here, with me, close to me. I need your warmth, I need your protection. Solitude will drive me crazy. Come, my love." She dragged him to her. Rami didn't resist. He clasped her strongly and crushed his lips against hers. Shlomit was very aroused; she didn't loosen her grip.

This hot passion, Rami thought to himself, may be the effect of alcohol or perhaps she is unconsciously taking her revenge and striking out at the man who, this day, ceased to be her father.

"Tonight, I will be your wife," she said, as she pulled open her blouse. Her swollen breasts were naked. Their erect nipples seemed to point enticingly at him. Excited, she panted, "Come Rami, Ra . . ha . . mim, come!"

Rami felt his heart beating wildly. He was breathless; blood rushed to his face. He could no longer remain unmoved before such beauty and under the powerful summons of his senses. Mechanically, he flicked the light switch and plunged the room into half-darkness. Then he undressed and leaped into bed.

Rami woke up early. He reached for his transistor radio, and the little set began to broadcast sweet, light music. Then he leaned over to his lover and gently placed a kiss on her lips. Shlomit opened her eyes and replied with a radiant smile. "Ah!" she exclaimed, stretching her arms and breathing in deeply. "I feel wonderful! As if I were reborn to a new life, a long life of love, together . . . with you."

They were both naked and looked at their bodies with admiration. Then Rami glanced at his watch. "I have to start getting ready," he said. "You too, and from now on, we'll go to the barracks together, every day."

"Yes, dear," she answered. "But it's still early. Let me savor these delicious moments a little longer. I feel completely renewed, like the phoenix arising from its ashes. Yesterday, I lost my identity; I no longer existed, I was reduced to cinders. Today, I've discovered a new and happier me; and this miraculous metamorphosis—you're the one who brought it about. It has come out of our union."

Rami was already out of bed, listening to her. Suddenly, he stopped and looked at the bedsheet. It was stained with blood. "Look," he said.

"Yes, I know," she said. "Rami dear, I am your wife, already your wife, without ceremony, without contract. We've sealed our union with the strongest of bonds, with blood."

"Yes darling, my wife, my beloved wife. We are united for better or for worse, until death do us part."

Their premarital union of the flesh had a therapeutic effect

91

on Shlomit, which surprised her "husband." He had never seen her so happy and so alive. On this first night, she had not only satisfied her sexual desires and acquainted herself with her sensuality, but by giving herself to Rahamim, she had also dealt a heavy blow at Mendel Weiss and at her false adoptive world. She had eagerly embraced what she felt was her native lineage, that wretched and despised Oriental tribe.

"When will we go to visit your family?" she asked, continuing her train of thought out loud.

"Next week if you wish."

"Good, I am anxious to see your father and what he represents. I think . . ."

"Next week, that is if . . ."

"If what?" she asked, troubled.

"If war doesn't break out," he answered nervously.

She blushed. She was supposed to know as much as he about the military tension on the borders and about the imminence of war. Still, she said, "Oh, no, not war! Not now that we're so happy!"

Rahamim paid no attention to her answer. "Sh . . . sh . . ." he said, "the news is on."

On the radio, the newscaster was announcing: "Kol Israel! The voice of Israel, from Jerusalem! Here is the latest news. President Nasser has just announced the blockade of the Straits of Tiran, and the interdiction of passage, in the Red Sea, to Israeli vessels. The Egyptian gunmen at Sharm-El-Sheik were ordered to fire at the first Israeli ship that attempts to break the blockade . . ."

"That's the end," Rami said, "there is no doubt any more. War is no longer a probability; it is now a certainty. Israel can't allow itself to be strangled without reacting. The generals cannot be restrained any more; the compressed steam of the military might will now be released and will unleash its formidable energy. We must get ready for the great misery of war, for the hundreds, perhaps the thousands of casualties. There will be more widows, more orphans, more bereaved parents."

"No, no," she cried, "the civilized world . . ."

92

"Please, don't be silly. The civilized world, as you call it, will not raise a finger. This is our war; this is our life; we . . ."

There was a loud knock at the door. Shlomit opened it, shivering. In front of her stood a sergeant with a message in his hand. "Is Lieutenant Levy here?" he asked.

"Yes, why?" Shlomit asked, although she instinctively knew.

"He must report to his unit immediately," replied the sergeant.

Just then Rami came out of the kitchen. "Lieutenant Levy," said the sergeant, "by order of the colonel, there is a jeep waiting for you downstairs. Please be ready in fifteen minutes."

The lieutenant put on his uniform. His bag was already packed.

Shlomit had tears in her eyes. "What a life!" she lamented. "Misfortune seems to dog my steps. My happiness hasn't even lasted one full day. Rami darling, I'm going to be all alone in this world. Be careful, my love, and come back alive!"

"Please, Shlomit, have a little more courage. I'm not the only one going to war. You'll stay at the base, even if we cross the border. Don't forget, you are our secretary and you will be the first to hear from me. If there is a pause in the action, I will call you from the front as soon as it can be done."

The lovers embraced a long time, their arms tightly wrapped around each other. Then they kissed good-bye, and the lieutenant quickly went down the stairs and hopped into the jeep which immediately set off at full speed.

The next day, Shlomit returned to her job at the military base. It was almost empty. Only a few women soldiers, secretaries like herself, were seated at their desks, very attentive to their radio sets. There were also a few soldiers and service officers, *jobnicks* as they were called, who stayed back at the base. Uri was one of them. He was cooling his heels in his office, furious at not being able to join his men in the paratroopers because of his health.

"What am I doing here like an idiot?" he grumbled. "The action isn't here, but there, at the border. Shlomit dear, do you know what that bastard of a doctor wrote when he reexamined me at my request? 'Unfit for combat.' That's a doctor? That's a cobbler! Who does he think he is? I'll appeal his decision."

Shlomit took heart at so much bravado from her superior officer. She didn't doubt his sincerity. "Don't get upset, Uri," she said, "you've already done your duty. It's your son's turn this time."

"Yes, my son Gadi is also an officer in the paratroopers. He'll give them hell!"

The very first night of their separation, Lieutenant Levy was sent with his unit to camp one mile from the Jordanian border. This "picnic," as the soldiers called it, lasted for thirteen days, a time full of anxiety. The ball was still in the courts of the diplomats. They hoped for a last-minute world intervention that would prevent armed conflict. The generals gnawed at the bit; they were afraid of losing their secret weapon, the element of surprise, and were also worried about the possible deterioration of the morale of their troops, most of whom were reservists, older men and fathers of families. Even worse, the people began to doubt the efficacy of the army and the competence of the government. The situation was fraught with danger. Encircled on all sides and threatened by extermination, abandoned to its fate by the "civilized world," the people of Israel once more found themselves compelled to go to war. Once again, there was no alternative. "*Ein Breira*," repeated the soldiers who had been ordered to carry the war beyond the border, to break the back of the enemy, and to destroy his military machine.

During the transition period, Shlomit didn't leave the military camp. This way, she could better follow the events which were unleashed with such dizzying speed. On two occasions, she had heard Rami's voice on the phone, but each time, it was very brief. Then, she lost all contact during the six days of the war. On the seventh day, the fighting stopped. Uri told Shlomit to get ready to go on a military assignment in occupied territory.

94

A hateful task was theirs to perform: they had to count the dead, wounded, and missing in action, and also to do an inventory of the enemy equipment destroyed and captured, or abandoned by the routed army. Several lists of casualties had already been reported. Rahamim Levy was not among them. Half-reassured but still quivering with fright, Shlomit got into the jeep beside Uri, and they set off for the hated mission.

Lieutenant Levy, apprised of their impending visit, waited impatiently for his wife. The newly conquered roads were not yet totally safe. In spite of the cease-fire, snipers still prowled the mountains and threatened foot soldiers and light vehicles. Levy also feared the jeep might go astray although he didn't doubt Uri's ability and sense of direction.

They arrived late that afternoon. Shlomit jumped out of the vehicle and threw her arms around her lover. She hadn't seen him for three weeks. She ran her hands up and down his body to assure herself that he was still alive and unharmed. She wept from joy and said over and over again, "I feared for your life; I don't know what I would have done if . . ."

"Darling, I was lucky," he said. "Three times I barely escaped death. There is a lot of chance in war and many of my buddies were killed simply because they were there, at the wrong place, at the wrong time. Now the war is over. We've won and the peace for which we've been waiting for so long has finally come. Our children will not have to suffer as we have."

Uri walked towards them. Despite his silence, Rami understood Uri's message. "Darling, you must have work to do. Here's Uri, waiting for you. Get on with it. I'll see both of you at dinner time."

The company received orders to stay put that day, and all the night. The armored column stretched over one mile along the road to Jericho. Officers and soldiers were relaxed. The danger was over; euphoria was at its height. The word *peace* was on everyone's lips. The future seemed bright; an era of brotherly cooperation between the Semitic peoples was on the horizon. Among the soldiers, discussion was very animated. They went on from peace to the occupied territories, and next, to the refugees.

"There they are," yelled a soldier looking in the direction of Jericho.

"Who?" asked his comrades.

Some men, through the conditioned reflex of soldiers at war fearing danger, instinctively fingered their triggers. But their buddy assured them, "I meant the refugees we were talking about. They're still off over there in the distance."

One of the officers adjusted his binoculars. "True, they are civilians walking on the side of the highway in a column that looks pretty long. We'll soon see. We'd better tell the commander."

It was dinner time. They'd already begun to distribute the combat rations. Uri and Shlomit came to join Rami's group. Their faces were drawn, their expressions serious. Not having taken part in the violent and murderous fights of the first two days of the war, they hadn't acclimated to the horrors and had not acquired the resignation in the face of death that immunized the combatants against the terrible shock of seeing their comrades-in-arms, so alive and vocal a few minutes earlier, reduced to bloody and motionless cadavers. Uri broke the unbearable silence: "That damn forced retirement has ruined me. In combat, you haven't got the time to think about what's happening. But by such garbling inactivity, drowning in the damn paper work that smells of death, how could I forget my dearest buddies with whom I fought side by side for ten years? How can I tell the horrible news to their wives and children, now widows and orphans. No, I can't look them in the eye . . . I . . ."

The group of refugees drew nearer. The commander's order was to let them come up and make a column, parallel to the armored column on the other side of the road, but not to let them cross over the line. Their fate would be decided later by the general.

The soldiers stopped all activity to look at their enemy. The scene upset them very badly. Shaking with fear, stood the real victims of the conflict. There were bent-over old men dressed in rags, a twisted branch in their hands serving as a cane. Their wrinkled wives were covered in black from head to toe, and carried in sacks on their backs their puny and almost naked babies. Some of the women balanced on their heads baskets which contained their meager possessions. Children constantly brushed away swarms of flies which covered their bodies, filthy bodies of skin and bones, and open sores oozing with blood and pus. Shlomit almost fainted at this sight; she couldn't help crying out, "It's a disgrace to humanity!" She had heard about wretchedness, poverty, ignorance, and the state of neglect of neighboring Arabs, but she had never imagined it to be like this. It was shocking to everybody. Soldiers who were courageous in facing enemy fire were now nauseated. Some even began to doubt the meaning of their own heroism.

"These are our enemies?" an officer wondered. "Is there any glory in conquering a people like this? What are we doing in this war? Where are their brothers who swore to exterminate us? Why don't they wage a war of extermination against poverty and lice, against ignorance and disease?"

The soldiers' curiosity was very strong. Several of them had never seen an Arab in their lives. No one could remain indifferent. Mixed groups formed, made up of refugees and soldiers. The soldiers made obvious efforts to gain the confidence of the frightened fugitives who expected to be massacred. When the oldest among them finally opened his mouth, he said that the entire group hadn't eaten for two days and that the children would die of hunger if they weren't given food right away. Then, he walked with halting steps toward the nearest tank and dramatically kissed the blue and white Star of David flag which was flapping in the wind. Then he stepped back a few steps, grabbed a portrait of the Jordanian king which had been captured in combat, and, to the amazement of the soldiers, spat on the image of his monarch. "Long live Israel! May Allah protect Israel!" he shouted as he returned to his group. "Long live Israel! May Allah protect Israel!" his unfortunate countrymen repeated.

The soldiers looked at them, obviously baffled. How many

mysteries this unknown and unfathomable newly conquered Orient held in store for them!

A heated argument broke out among the soldiers: Should they give their combat food rations to the poor starving people? "No," said a corporal, "you don't know these people. They are tricky. First of all, how do we know if the old man was not lying? We are not sure that they haven't eaten for two days. Secondly, they're not prisoners of war, there's nothing that says we have to feed our enemies and deprive ourselves of our rations. Thirdly, and if the war were to start again . . ."

"How can you talk that way?" his amazed buddy asked. "I left three children at home. Almost all of us are fathers of families. Do you have the heart to let these children starve to death?"

"Think a little about it, my friend," said a third soldier. "If the shoe were on the other foot, if they were the conquerors, there would not be any one of us left alive, not a woman, not a child. Remember the classified document that our unit captured, which contained the order to the Jordanian army to occupy Motza and kill everyone there, men, women, and children?"

"If we acted like them," replied his friend, "Israel would no longer have a reason for existence. Deprived of our moral strength, we would become another Levantine state like our neighbors. What you are suggesting is against our fathers' teaching, against our law, against our customs. These poor wretched people have done nothing. They aren't responsible for the war."

One of the officers came to his aid: "Our war," he said, "is a defensive war. Our goal is the destruction of the enemy's military power which has threatened to exterminate us. We have nothing against the Arab peoples whose greatest enemies are their own leaders. Let's not demean our struggle. Feeding these hungry people is a purely humanitarian act."

This lively argument didn't last for long. Some soldiers went from words to deeds and gave their own food rations to the refugee families facing them. Their action triggered a continuous flow of soldiers carrying food from the mighty armored column to the hungry human column. In a few minutes, all of the provisions had been handed out. The soldiers returned to their vehicles.

The refugees, grouped in families, ate ravenously. Their voracity was the best proof of the old man's veracity. As he ate, the patriarch waved his hands and made frantic gestures of gratitude. When they finished their meal, the refugees arose and new mixed groups formed. They were more at ease one with the other. The refugees were relaxed; fear disappeared from their faces. Some Arabic speaking soldiers went over to the old man. Rami was among them, followed by Shlomit for whom he translated as the conversation proceeded.

The old man raised his hands to the sky and thanked Allah for letting him come through alive, with his family and his group. He recounted their story:

"We left Jericho two days ago to escape the Israeli army because our leaders told us over and over again that we would all be massacred by the Jews. We hoped we would catch up with the king's army, but instead of that, we fell into your hands. We thought that our doom was sealed but we found just the opposite. Not only have you spared our lives, but you gave us your own food. We don't know what to say. Allah must certainly be with you. That's why you have won this war. Long live Israel! Allah be with Israel!"

"Long live Israel, Allah be with Israel!" his companions echoed.

"Are you all from Jericho?" asked Rami.

"I, your humble servant, was born in Jericho and I know no other city. This is the first time in my life that I have left Jericho. But here, a little farther away, there are a few families who have suffered a whole lot more than we, and who have been homeless for twenty years. They live in a refugee camp near Jericho. They say that their homes and their lands are in Palestine, and that one day, they will return to them. They are the ones who urged us to run away. It is because of them that we are here, under God's protection and yours."

99

The old man paused for a moment; then he began to yell, pointing at one of the Palestinian refugees: "Ya Amin, taalahon! Come here, Amin!"

All heads turned towards the man whom the patriarch had just called. He was startled but repressed the instinctive movement of his head. He didn't even deign to answer. "The poor fellow," said the old man, "he has been blind for many years. Come with me; let us go see him."

The whole group followed him. Amin was really blind and he insisted on playing the deaf-mute. He hadn't touched his food ration which remained intact at his side. "Why haven't you eaten, Amin?" the old man asked. "You must be hungry like everybody else."

"I will take nothing from the hands of the Jews, these cursed people who have stolen my house, my land, my daughter, my Jihada!" shouted the blind man with bitter anger. "The war is not yet over, and we will hurl them all into the sea. You, Sheik Ahmed, you are a traitor and you will be hanged. They can kill me if they want to, I have nothing more to lose; tfooh!" The man spat with contempt, and although he didn't reach anyone, his gesture was enough to make everybody recoil.

Sheik Ahmed went back to his place, followed by the entire group. "He has always been this way, hateful and hated by all," he said. "It's true that he has had a very hard and unfortunate life, but it's also his fault. Before the first war, when he lived at Om-El-Kokeb, he was a soldier in the Kaukdji battalions. Then in 1948 he fled from Palestine, abandoned his home and his land, and they say that he even left there a little girl, a baby. We heard that she was living in a kibbutz. His first wife, the baby's mother, died in childbirth. The second died in Jericho. That I saw with my own eyes. Two of his sons were killed as *fedayeen*. The rest of his family is now scattered around, and he doesn't know where they are. A few years ago, Amin Ibn-Hussein got married for the third time, but his wife deserted him a few weeks after the wedding because she couldn't stand his character and because he didn't provide for her needs. You see the kind of life that Allah wanted for this miserable man."

Amin Ibn-Hussein's story aroused the interest of the audience. Shlomit very nervously followed the translation by Rami, who was himself stunned by his account. "All this," he said, "is the result of war which breeds suffering on both sides. The most amazing thing is that this man, who has lost everything because of the war, does not seem happy to see its end."

"It's precisely because he lost everything that he has nothing more to lose," answered Shlomit. "But what I can't understand is how it is possible to abandon a child and then do nothing to regain her. After all, we are not savages."

Rami translated Shlomit's question for the old Sheik; the old man's answer was very quick: "Amin was always on the run, in the mountains, in the desert. He left his poor wife with seven children without resources. She died of it. The International Red Cross sent representatives to ask her to take the child back but she refused. She couldn't add to her already unbearable burden."

A few minutes later, the company commander received two orders. The first was to get the refugees on military trucks and return them home, to Jericho. The second was for the whole company to make a U-turn, at dawn, and head towards the North, to the recently conquered Golan Heights, in order to relieve another company which was cut to bits by the bloody combat of the previous days.

The next morning, at daybreak, the trucks were already back from Jericho, and Shlomit and Uri headed for the base. As for the combatants, they were in a gloomy mood. They had thought the war was over and that peace was at hand. The unexpected order to go up North was disconcerting. Shlomit suffered the most. This new separation tormented her very much. The period of euphoria was very brief. The story of the poor blind man, in spite of his hatred and his inflammatory oaths, shook her to the depths of her being. She was seized with pity and sorrow for his unfortunate daughter because she herself had been abandoned by her real parents and adopted by strangers. But by an instinctive reaction which, paradoxically, makes it easier to resign to misfortune shared by others,

Shlomit began to accept the fact of her adoption. It even occurred to her that she might one day break her vow and visit her parents, with the hope of effecting a reconciliation, even a partial one. She would forget the past, she thought, if only Mendel Weiss would agree to her marriage with Rahamim. Still, she decided to postpone her visit to the Weisses until her lover returned from war. She would stay at the base from which she could talk to him every day by a direct telephone line recently installed.

One day, sitting idle at her desk, Shlomit was startled by the ringing of the phone, fearfully anticipating bad news. But she recovered her calm when she heard Rami's voice. "I have a weekend pass," he said. "What about going to visit my parents, as I promised you?"

"Gladly," she answered. "I will stay all day at the barracks, waiting for you."

Chapter Fifteen

The Oriental market in Ramleh began to quiet down after the noisy hubbub of Thursday afternoon and Friday morning. Several housewives were still standing in front of the almost-empty stalls, looking for a last-minute bargain. On Friday afternoon, the tired merchants, anxious to get home before the Sabbath, got rid of what was left of their wares at ridiculous prices. Some were pulling down their sliding metal doors; others were cleaning up their shops with powerful jets of water gushing out of rubber hoses.

Rabbinas ran a little shop at the market. The trade in fruit and vegetables, though very profitable, wasn't his line. He didn't have the strength for it. He was happy about what he called "a little hole in the wall," a kind of kiosk which supplied the merchants with cigarettes and refreshing drinks, and the children with all kinds of candy. The little hole provided his daily bread, literally. He was no longer dependent on his son. Moreover, the hole made it possible for him to rebuild a miniature version of his world of yesteryear. Of course, there was no longer a Sheik Sliman. But a padded cushioned chair, set between the hole and the street, was always occupied by a guest. The setting was different, the subjects of conversation of another order, but wisdom and a philosophical atmosphere still reigned in Rabbinas's little shop.

A few years earlier, when his son David got married, Rabbinas had decided to leave Hadera for a peaceful and inexpensive spot where he could live with people of his own kind.

Ramleh was indeed an ideal place. There, he found a synagogue that welcomed him, people of his own age, immigrants from North Africa with whom he was able to communicate, and a social environment in which he was free to live according to his own habits. He had succeeded in marrying off his daughter Sarah rather young in order to protect her, as he said, from the temptations of sin. This marriage greatly reduced his expenses and his worries. "Your mother and I are old," he had said to David, urging him to get married and observe the *mitsvah* of increase and multiply.' " We need very little, and it is time to think of yourself and your future."

David often came with his wife to visit his parents. Sarah didn't live far from Ramleh, and her parents saw her every day. Only Rahamim was a rare visitor. First his studies, then his military service completely monopolized him. Rabbinas rejoiced whenever his younger son surprised him with a short call to inquire about his health. Rabbinas proudly kept account of his son's academic achievements and of his success in the army. "He is under God's protection," he would often tell his worried wife to allay her fears. During the general mobilization, David, too, was away somewhere in the Sinai Desert, and Sarah, whose husband was also drafted, moved temporarily to her father's house.

Rabbinas hadn't seen Rahamim for more than a month. On two occasions, he had received news of him through a fellow soldier. The last time, it was on the seventh day of the war and the message set his mind at ease. Three weeks had passed by since then. As he did every day, he raised his eyes to Heaven to beg God for mercy, for "*rahamim*." He recalled the ceremony of circumcision, back during the Nazi occupation.

"Rahamim, Rahamim," he implored God, "that's the name I gave him. Have mercy on us!" Then he took the book of Psalms out of his drawer and began to read: "The Lord will hear thee in the day of distress . . ."

A little boy entered, stopped a moment, and looked at Rabbinas with eyes full of veneration. Then he put a small coin in a plate and, out of a cardboard box, took a chocolate bar which he began to nibble as he left. Rabbinas sensed the presence of the child but he paid no attention to this strange transaction. People in the neighborhood were convinced that this man of God prayed for all of them, and that it would be dangerous to interrupt his prayers or his reading of the Scriptures. Children were warned by their elders of the misfortune that would befall them if they gave in to temptation and stole from this holy man.

After reading two chapters of the Psalms, Rabbinas paused and sighed. A young soldier stood in front of him. The old man felt his heart beat faster. "God," he murmured, "what news?"

"Are you Rabbinas Levy?" the soldier asked, gazing rapidly around the narrow confines of this hole in the wall.

"Yes, I am. Is everything all right?"

"Rahamim asked me to tell you that he would be home this evening with his fiancée. I promised him that I would be here ahead of him, but unfortunately I was delayed. Has he already arrived?"

"Not yet," replied the holy man. "Thank you, my son. God bless you," answered Rabbinas. Then he immediately closed the door and headed for home to break the good news to his wife.

"His fiancée?" she wondered. "But we never participated in his engagement."

"We will tonight. Let us thank God that he is safe and sound and that we will soon see him," said Rabbinas.

A few minutes before the Sabbath, Rahamim and Shlomit got off the bus. "You won't believe this," said Shlomit, "but I've never set foot in Ramleh. It's the first time I've seen this city which is so close to Tel Aviv."

"I don't know much more than you do about it," answered Rahamim. "I don't come here often!"

They walked down a wide paved road, bordered by tall buildings. "This section we're crossing is the new city, built after 1948," Rahamim said. "But if we want to get home faster and not be late for the *kidush*, we had better take a shortcut across the old Arab section of the town."

Shlomit patiently followed him, amazed at the condition of the streets which were narrow, unasphalted and lined with walls that were falling down. It wasn't even a dirt road; at each step, a heavy cloud of dust rose into the air.

"This is the old city," announced Rahamim. "During the 1948 war, its inhabitants fled and became refugees like those we met the other day near Jericho. As a matter of fact, that wicked old blind man who deserted his daughter is originally from a village not far from here."

"Oh, yes," said Shlomit, pensive. Memories from that day came to her. In her imagination she saw the poor blind man and that whole column of starving and terrified refugees. The picture of the abandoned baby haunted her. After a moment of hesitation, she asked apprehensively, "Do your parents live in an Arab house?"

Rahamim was surprised by the question, but nevertheless, he answered: "Arab, yes. House, no. They have a room and kitchen privileges in an Arab house which they share with several North African immigrant families. It is better for them this way. They feel more at home, their expenses are reduced, and they are not far from the business—I mean the little kiosk my father runs in the marketplace."

He stopped walking to observe his companion's reactions. Her eyes had the same empty, sad look that had bothered him on the night of their prenuptial union. "What are you thinking of?" he asked. "I told you that my parents weren't wealthy, and you know all about my background."

Shlomit got hold of herself and replied shyly: "No, dear. It's not that. I thought of our strange world, how people build houses, and others come and live in them, simply because they happen to be on the right side."

"Fine! You think that you've just discovered America," he said ironically. "You had to come to Ramleh to find that . . ."

"No! No!" interrupted Shlomit. "Since the other day, near Jericho, it was the scene with the refugees that made this tragedy more real to me, more tangible."

"Take it easy, Shlomit. Nobody chased those refugees from

their homes. They were following the orders of their leaders who promised a quick victory, one week at the most, and a big booty of houses, jewels and women after they threw the Jews into the sea."

"Do you really believe that?" Shlomit asked.

"Do you still have any doubt after what we've been through in this war?"

"No, Rami, I know, but it is always the innocent who suffer."

"War!" Rami exclaimed, "war is a horrible thing, and as long as they think they can win, there will be no peace in our area. And the innocent, as you say, will continue to suffer."

"War," Shlomit repeated, "the great invention of human stupidity."

"Here we are," said Rami, relieved to end the conversation. Shlomit stopped for a moment. "Is there anything I should know? This is a new environment for me. How should I act?"

"As naturally as possible. Be yourself, Shlomit Weiss, daughter of . . ." Rami swallowed his spittle, aware of his *faux pas*, and blushed a bit.

Shlomit followed up to ease her companion's embarrassment: "of Mendel and Gita Weiss," she said, stressing each word.

When the couple entered, there was tremendous joy for the whole family. An atmosphere of harmony and serenity filled the room. It was Friday evening, and in Rabbinas's house, Queen Sabbath was solemnly welcomed and revered. The bed was covered with a clean, brightly colored sheet. A white tablecloth was laid on the small dining table in the middle of the room. Two Sabbath lights flickered in a corner, and the scent of sweet perfume filled the air.

Esther Levy kissed her son and his fiancée. Rabbinas hugged Rahamim and shook Shlomit's hand. Then he recited the prayer of *hagomel*, thanking God for having saved his son from the dangers of war. When he finished, he turned to his son and asked him bluntly, "Rahamim, my son, did you kill in the war?"

"No, Father," answered the lieutenant, "it may be hard to

107

believe, but during the six days of the war, I didn't fire a single shot."

"Thank God!" sighed the old man.

Shlomit was overwhelmed with such humanity and wisdom. Rabbinas understood her astonishment. "Yes, my daughter," he said, "this war was not wanted by Israel. Defending ourselves is not only a right but a duty, because life is sacred. It is a gift of God, and He alone, blessed-be-His-name, can take it away. Our law commands us, 'He who comes to kill you, kill him first,' but if we can escape danger and beat our enemy without killing, God is still more pleased, since the enemy is also made in His image."

"Yes, yes, Mr. Levy," stammered Shlomit, amazed.

"You can call me Father, as Rahamim does. And you, my daughter, what is your name?"

"Shlomit," she said, "Shlomit Weiss."

"Shlomit?" the old man repeated. "That's a very pretty name. I hope it will bring us the *shalom*, the peace we crave for with all our hearts. You said 'Wa-yess?' What is it?"

Rahamim came to her rescue: "Father," he said, "Weiss is German and also Yiddish, and it means *white*."

"Yiddish!" exclaimed his mother. "So your fiancée is *voosvoos*! But she is brown-skinned and dark-haired. She looks like one of us."

"It makes no difference, Mother," Rahamim said firmly.

Rabbinas nodded his head, agreeing with his son. "We're all Jews, Esther, don't forget," he admonished his wife. "All of Israel are holy people, *voosvoos*, or African, there is no difference. What really matters is that Shlomit is Jewish, born in the law of Moses."

This verdict was final and Rabbinas asked for the wine for the *kidush* before the Sabbath meal. On his father's signal, Rahamim covered his head and stood up. The old man intoned the prayer, and his son followed him in a lower voice: "On the sixth day, God completed heaven and earth and all the work of the creation . . . He rested on the seventh day . . . which he blessed and sanctified . . ."

When the prayer was over, Rabbinas drank from the wine and passed the glass to Rahamim, who did the same. Then, his mother took a swallow and gave the half-empty glass to her future daughter-in-law.

"Six days!" marveled Rabbinas, "It took six days for God to create all the universe. It also took six days for the Israeli forces to win the war and save the people from destruction. Now may we rest from war and have eternal peace!"

He then cut the Sabbath bread and muttered the *hamotsi* prayer of gratitude to God for making the land give bread. He gave each one of the family a piece of bread dipped in salt. This last rite signaled the beginning of the meal. Throughout the religious ceremony, Shlomit felt as a stranger. Mendel Weiss had never recited the *kidush*, or the *hamotsi*. She was also apprehensive of the exotic dishes, whose hot Oriental spices she was already smelling. When she was served, she made tremendous efforts not to embarrass her hosts, helping herself between mouthfuls to long gulps of water to cool off the oily hot foods which she swallowed in small doses. Rami himself had lost his taste for his mother's cooking and he could hardly keep down the heavy, biting sauces. They nonetheless did their best to please the parents.

When the meal was over, Rahamim got up and told Shlomit that they had to leave. His mother was unhappy with the short visit. "Have you already set your marriage date? When will we see Shlomit's parents? Where are you going to live?" she inquired anxiously. Rahamim interrupted her questioning, saying that nothing had been decided yet, and that they would keep them posted.

Rabbinas called the couple over and placed a hand on each head to give them his blessing. When he finished, Rahamim kissed his father's hand. Shlomit hesitated a moment, then did the same, and they left the house, followed by their neighbors' curious looks.

It was very late when the couple got back to their room. They had not been together since their "wedding night." The war had separated them, and the long absence had sharpened their desires. They thirsted for each other and were determined to devote the weekend to their love.

"Our honeymoon was interrupted by the war," Rahamim said.

"Tonight, we will avenge ourselves of the war!" she replied, as she slipped completely naked between the cool white sheets.

Rami finished undressing. "And what a vengeance, my darling!" he exclaimed. Then, he turned off the lights and joined the quivering body of his beloved young wife.

They were slow to wake up. It was Saturday, and the quiet atmosphere of the Sabbath contributed to their pleasant indolence. Shlomit opened her eyes and tenderly kissed her bedmate's lips. He woke up. "Ah!" he said, drawing her into his arms, "I have lost the habit of sleeping late. It's great, particularly when you're in my arms."

"We have the whole day ahead of us," answered Shlomit. Then she added: "Darling, I thought a lot before waking you up."

"About what? The war?"

"No, about us and our future."

"And what was the result of your long think?" the young man inquired somewhat skeptically.

"I noticed yesterday," she said, "a kind of uneasiness in your parents. I don't know if it has a religious basis, but I understood that they were not happy about our long engagement and that they would like to see us already married."

"I think you're right. Well, aren't we married? Aren't you my wife? Haven't we sworn fidelity to each other on an oath of blood? What else is there to do?"

"No, no, I am thinking about marriage, as everybody else does. I mean . . . the ceremony, the contract, the whole bit . . ."

"Shlomit darling, have you considered both sides of the situation? Aren't you aware that the war is not yet over and that I am still on garrison duty on the Golan Heights and that every night we repel attacks and soldiers continue to get hit? I have no contract with death, you know, and if the worst were to happen to me, I wouldn't want to leave a widow behind me, with a contract . . ."

"Oh, Rami darling, with or without a contract, you are the only man in my life . . . But . . . it's not for me . . . it's for him," she said, pointing at her belly.

"What?" exclaimed Rami, "Am I to understand that . . ."

Shlomit nodded her head.

"And you've hidden the news from me deliberately?"

"Please forgive me, dear. I didn't know until yesterday when I saw the doctor and I didn't want to spoil the evening with your parents. I am the one who has suffered the most for keeping this secret one more day."

"Shlomit, my adorable wife, I don't know whether I should rejoice or grieve at the news. I would have preferred to become the father of your child under different circumstances, but we must shoulder our responsibilities and stand up to this new situation. After all, most of the army in war is made up of fathers. I will be one of them. Besides, you will be discharged. You will be a lovely, loving mother."

"I am anxious to get rid of this uniform and I am looking forward to becoming a tender mother . . . and a good house-wife."

"Good, my darling. I still wish you had told me the news before we visited my parents. It would have saved me a second trip and ended their worries. Anyhow, I will go see them as soon as possible. As for your parents . . ."

Shlomit trembled and looked at him, amazed at his words.

Rami added, a little embarrassed, "I mean the Weisses, you will have to decide what to do with them . . . It's your . . ."

"But your mother!" Shlomit interrupted.

"Never mind my mother; it's none of her business. Do what you see fit."

"You heard her. She wants to see my parents. I know it will cause your folks a great deal of pain if their son marries a girl who has no family. Worst of all, they will ask for an expla-nation . . ."

"Well then?"

"I will make a last effort with the Weisses. Maybe Mendel has changed. This war has altered many mentalities; the miraculous victory, after the great danger of extermination, may have brought hearts closer . . ."

"If that is true, your parents, or rather the Weisses, should have tried to seek you out. They know very well where you are."

"They're probably ashamed, or even sick. Who knows?"

"Do as you wish, my darling."

"What do you think about going there this evening? You're off until tomorrow morning."

"Oh no, I will not go without being invited, and welcomed. I would like to forget the scene of the other night, but I don't want any more humiliation."

"I understand, darling," Shlomit said. "I think I know the answer; I will go visit them and you will wait quietly on a bench in the park across the street. If I don't return in a quarter of an hour, you will come over, and the three of us will greet you at the door. Will you do that for me?"

"Fine. Your plan is very ingenious, my dear, like a mystery story. You planned it like a military operation. I will faithfully carry it out, watch in hand."

Chapter Sixteen

It was five o'clock in the afternoon when the couple arrived in Tel Aviv. As they had agreed, Rahamim went over to the park while Shlomit headed towards the Weiss's apartment. She was very nervous; her heart was pounding, and she felt her knees quake under her. Hesitatingly, she walked toward the unknown and continuously rehearsed the words she would say and the gestures that would help relax the atmosphere and make communication with her "parents" easier. Once she got in the entrance, she hurried, lowering her head to avoid meeting any of the neighbors who might impede her way and ask her a heap of embarrassing questions about her private life and her relationship with her parents. The military uniform she wore preserved her anonymity in that post-war period when passers-by in uniform were more common than people in civilian clothes. When she had climbed a few stairs, she grew more and more anxious. Her throat was dry, and a heavy load was pressing on her chest, making her breathing extremely painful. Her hands were wet with sweat, and a cold perspiration flowed down her spine. All of a sudden, she felt dizzy and clutched the handrail to avoid falling and losing consciousness. She tried to reassure herself, attributing this sickness to her first pregnancy, but even when she recovered, a terrible fear overcame her.

She climbed up the stairs, her two damp hands still grasping the handrail, and she soon found herself facing the door which was half-open. She hesitated a moment. Would she knock at the door or would she surprise them? But the ill-fated young woman didn't have to make a choice. Sharp screams and jerking sobs came from inside the apartment. Her curiosity was compelling. She turned her ear and then her whole body towards the deafening noise and finally entered the hall, unnoticed, and stood there, frozen with fright. They were quarreling about her. Up until then, she had only known that she was adopted. When she decided to return that day, it was with the intention to "adopt" them, in a deliberate and conciliatory act, as her "true" parents. But what she now discovered stopped her cold.

Gita's nervous whines pierced her ears. Her eardrums pounded, and she could hardly discern. "Here I am, sick and dying," said the unfortunate woman, her voice shaking with repeated gasps. "I will never forgive you for having separated me from the only one in the world that I love, from my daughter, from Shlomit."

"She isn't your daughter and you know it," yelled her husband. "If she were our real daughter, she wouldn't have left us in this way. We gave her everything; we spoiled her, we coddled her, we educated her. We raised her for eighteen years and we made all sacrifices. And this is our reward! What an ungrateful child!"

Shlomit wanted to interrupt him, to burst into the room and scream: "No, I didn't abandon you, I am not ungrateful; here I am, I am home, I adopt you of my own free will. You are my real, my only parents, I'm going to get married. I am going to have a baby . . ." But she checked herself; out of pride, or maybe because of an instinctive curiosity, she didn't budge. She stood there, motionless, breathing heavily. She wanted to know more.

"No," Gita sobbed, "you gave her nothing. All that you've done is for yourself, to satisfy your own whim and vanity."

"For myself?" Mendel yelled. "Not for you, no, not because of your damned barrenness! If I'd married another woman, I would have had my own children; I wouldn't have adopted this bitch, this . . . foreigner."

"Stop it, you cruel man! That poor girl, you have deprived her of her most cherished possession, of her identity. You insisted on keeping her background from her; you stole her from her own people."

"Her own people! What does she mean?" Shlomit muttered between her chattering teeth. "God, am I not of this people? Am I not Jewish? It's impossible, I can't believe my ears!"

Mendel's voice went on hammering on the poor girl's head: "How dare you say that? That's too much!" He angrily banged his fist on the table. "What more do you want? Wasn't it enough to tell her that we had adopted her? Should we have revealed the truth about her origins, her real people, her real name? Should we have told her: 'Daughter, you are an Arab; your real name is Jihada, Jihada Ibn-Hussein. Your parents abandoned you when they fled from their village, and they refused to take you back, and they are now refugees in Jericho.' Is that . . ."

"Eeeeeh!!!"

A strident scream split the air, jolting Mendel and Gita who thought they were alone in the apartment. They ran towards the vestibule and found Shlomit lying on the floor, unconscious, a white foam on the corner of her lips. Her eyes were open but were sightless. Her hands and feet were feverishly shaking. Violent spasms contorted her face, and horrible convulsions twisted her body as if she were ravaged by poison. One word only came from her mouth, which she repeated tirelessly: "Jihada! . . . Jihada!"

Mendel and Gita were bewildered. They stood dumb and exchanged desperate looks. Suddenly they had forgotten their quarrel and were joined in an effort to help their daughter.

Gita brought a glass of water; she tried desperately to make her daughter drink, but Shlomit's teeth were clenched tight.

Mendel Weiss was at bay. After vainly walking back and forth, he sat in a corner, locked in meditation, his head buried in between his fists, eaten up with remorse. A stream of pictures flowed before his closed eyes. He saw himself as the conquering sergeant saving the life of an enemy's child abandoned by her own people. At that time, he was far from thinking that this deed which he believed to be so humane would have such cruel consequences for himself and his wife and might be fatal to the

115

child. "We must call a doctor," he said, breaking the painful silence that seemed to last forever, "or an ambulance."

"An ambulance? What for? Where is Shlomit?" Rami asked as he rushed in. He had waited a quarter of an hour as agreed before leaving the park. He was sure that Shlomit had made up with her family and he saw himself on the way to the altar. But when he arrived at the door, no one was there to greet him. He interpreted the deadly silence as an ominous foreboding, and Mendel's words confirmed his fears. Mendel was shocked at the sight of the unexpected visitor. He couldn't utter a word; he merely pointed to the poor, sick girl stretched out on the floor, whose name he avoided pronouncing. Her convulsive movements were now hardly visible.

Gita limped out of the kitchen where she was making some tea for the girl. As soon as she saw the officer, she ran towards him and hugged him. It was her way of sharing her sorrow with the young man. Then, painfully, she told him what had happened: her violent arguments with Mendel and the horrible, inadvertent revelations that had brought on such disastrous results.

Rami remained speechless for a few seconds, totally overwhelmed by what he had just learned. Then, he got down on the floor beside his wife, the mother of his still embryonic child, and covered her with hot kisses. But she was unconscious to his touch.

"I'm calling a military ambulance," he said, looking for the telephone. When he came back, he took up his place again at his wife's side. She seemed a little calmer. A few minutes later, she asked for a drink. Rami hurried to the kitchen and brought the glass of tea that Gita had prepared earlier.

Shlomit sat up and emptied the glass in one gulp. "More!" she commanded. Rami obeyed, his hope rising. This insatiable thirst, he thought, was a sure sign of recovery. "Where am I?" she asked, looking inquisitively at the walls and doors of the apartment.

Rami tried to get his answer through: "You are here, with me, your husband, Rami, Rahamim." But it was to no avail; she

116

was not listening, she could not listen. "Take it easy, darling," he added. "You'll see, you'll be all right."

"Where am I? Who am I?" the sick girl persisted. The second question shook Rahamim to the core.

"God, she has lost her memory!" he exclaimed, turning toward the old couple who were as upset as he. Mendel and Gita had let him take care of her without interfering. They were sure he could do much better than they, because the girl felt only love for him.

Rahamim took a step toward her. Shlomit recoiled, screaming: "Ji-ha-da, Ji-ha-da, Ji . . ."

Holding back his tears, the young officer uttered, "Whoever you are, you are my wife, Shlom . . . Jihada. You are the only woman I have ever loved. You will get well; we will get married; we will leave the army . . ."

The last word excited her rage. She savagely pulled the buttons off her military blouse and hurled them away, one after the other, with screams of horror. Then she ripped off the shirt and the skirt which made up her military uniform and threw them, rumpled up, into the air, as if to exorcise her grief-stricken body of the last shreds of a false identity which she had assumed for nineteen years. The ritual stripping down went on with obscene gestures and sharp, jerky cries alternated with short, violent fits of wild laughter.

Rami was seized by pity for Shlomit. It seemed to him that she had lost control of herself. There was nothing more he could do but wait for the ambulance. With tears running along his cheeks, he contemplated the almost naked body, which he had adored and which was now in tatters. She was shivering. He entered one of the rooms, looking for a blanket. When he came back, she was no longer there. Rami dropped the blanket and went off running to the door. She was already outside at the foot of the stairs. Sensing danger, the young man raced down the stairs, four at a time, and flew out of the building, puffing, looking in every direction.

A deafening shriek of brakes froze him on the spot. In a

117

bound, he crossed the sidewalk and landed by the side of a bus whose driver had just stepped down.

"She threw herself right under the wheels," the driver said. "It was suicide!"

Rami spotted the ambulance that he had called earlier and motioned it over to stop. They picked up her body, covered it with a blanket, and took off at top speed for the nearest hospital.

Mendel and Gita, informed by their neighbors, went right away to the emergency room. Gita could hardly walk. As she limped into the room, her face livid, her hands shaking, Rami jumped toward her and helped her to his seat. "Thank you, my son," she said. Mendel followed and sat beside his wife. An ominous silence reigned in the waiting room, disrupted only by Gita's frequent moans and sighs and the monotonous tick-tock of the old clock.

Suddenly, the door opened and the surgeon on duty entered. Rami walked toward him. "Doctor! How. . . ?"

The doctor invited him into his office. "I have just come from the operating room," he said. "Is she your wife?"

"Yes . . . no . . . we were going to get married soon."

"I'm sorry, lieutenant, she lost a lot of blood; she lost the baby."

"How is she?" Rami inquired.

"Critical, very critical," said the surgeon. "We're doing all we can to save her life. I suggest you all go home and get some sleep for tonight."

Rami shared the last part of the message with the Weisses. "You look tired," he added, "you should go home and rest for a few hours. I will stay here."

Mendel glanced at his wife. Gita nodded her head, "No," she whispered, "we will wait . . . with you."

At dawn Rahamim was called to the surgeon's office. "There has been a very slight improvement," the doctor said with caution, "but she is still in serious condition. There is still a great danger of postsurgical complications. She is now in the recovery room. You may see her for a few minutes, no more."

Rami regained some hope. The recovery room was open.

With velvet tread, he approached Shlomit's bed and sat beside her. When she opened her eyes, he exulted: "Shlomit, my. . . !" he exclaimed. She did not respond. "Shlomit!" he repeated, slightly raising the tone of his voice.

"No!" she whispered. "Ji-ha-da . . . Jericho . . . blind . . . my father . . . Arab . . . Ji-ha-da . . . Ji-ha-da . . ."

"Yes, Jihada, I love you. You are my wife, Jihada."

"No . . . not Jewish . . . no law . . . Mo . . . ses," she said, echoing Rabbinas's words.

"Jewish or not, what does it matter? We will go away from here, far away to another country. We will start a new life . . ."

"Life! . . . No . . . not crippled . . . better dead . . ."

Rami was terrified by this revelation. "But . . . the doctor . . ." he objected. Furtively, the nurse entered the room. She bent over him and said in a low voice, "The doctor asked you to please leave the room; she needs a lot of rest."

Rahamim came closer to Jihada who was already asleep. He kissed her on the forehead and returned to the waiting room. The inquisitive looks of the old couple embarrassed him: "Still very serious," he said, to preempt any questions.

Seven long hours passed that seemed an eternity. In the afternoon, the chief military nurse came with the horrible news: "I am very sorry," she said, "we have done everything possible, but we couldn't save her life. A blood clot killed her . . . so young, so beautiful." After a pause, she added, "We didn't find any papers, or documents . . . would you please come and identify her?"

The three of them followed the nurse into the operating room. She pulled back the sheet which covered Shlomit's face. "Who is she?" asked the nurse. "What is her name?"

Mendel and Gita looked simultaneously at the officer and seemed to await his verdict. He couldn't endure their tearful and imploring gaze. He lowered his eyes, did an about-face, and started toward the door. As he walked out, he heard Gita say, "She's our daughter. Her name is . . . Shlomit, Shlomit . . . Weiss."

119

Rami got back to his room. He glanced furtively at his desk. There was a paper there for his signature. He spotted a red pencil, grabbed it angrily, and covered the entire sheet with two letters: NO. He had just said no to the army. No, he didn't wish to reenlist. To hell with promotion, salary, scientific career. He had just lost all that he held dear in this world.

A feeling of emptiness pervaded him. "War!" he heard himself yell. "War is the great invention of human stupidity." Those were her words. Never had they sounded so real to him. No, he would not reenlist, but he would continue to fight, to fight against wars, to fight for peace between the two peoples. He owed it to Shlomit; he owed it to Jihada. He would live for her, and she would never die.

Glossary of Foreign Words and Expressions Used in This Novel

Beth Hamikdash: Jewish Holy Temple in Jerusalem
dahak: underpaid labor for unskilled workers
ein breira: there is no choice, no alternative
Eretz-Israel: the land of Israel, Palestine before independence
faux pas: a bad step, a mistake
fedayeen: guerrilla fighters
galuth: exile, state of the Jews in the Diaspora
hamotsi: a Hebrew prayer to thank God for giving us bread
jihad: holy war of the Moslems against the infidels
kefia: an Arab head covering of white cloth with a black circle on it
kidush: the Jewish prayer before the Sabbath and holiday meals
maarav: Hebrew word for "west"
Maghreb: Arabic word for "west"; general name for the three countries of North Africa: Tunisia, Algeria, Morocco
mazel tov: Hebrew greeting for "good luck"
mezuzah: a little glass tube containing a parchment with the name of God, usually fixed on the lintel of a door in Jewish homes
minian or *minyan*: a group of ten males required to pray together
mitsvot, plural of *mitsva*: a commandment, a good deed
mohel: the religious man who performs the circumcision
Mufti: high religious Moslem leader
nouveaux riches: newly rich people, generally through speculation or political favoritism

121

protecsia or *protectsia*: political favoritism

rahamim: pity, mercy

sabras: native born of Israel

savlanut: patience

shalom: peace

shehehiyanu: lit. "who kept us alive," a prayer to thank God for keeping us alive to see an important event

talith: a prayer shawl

tefillin: phylacteries, leather stripes and small boxes containing the name of God, used by Jews during the morning prayer

voosvoos: common nickname for the East-European Jews, given to them by the non-Ashkenazi immigrants; from "voos," Yiddish for "what"